THE

THE BACK END
OF NOWHERE

Jenny Sullivan

PONT BOOKS

First Impression—February 1997

ISBN 1 85902 497 1

This book is published with the support
of the Arts Council of Wales.

Printed in Wales at
Gomer Press, Llandysul, Ceredigion

For my parents—
Phyllis and the late Fred Anderson, with love.
Thank you so much for having me!
For my husband, Rob, for everything
and my daughters for their encouragement.
But this time, also for 'my class'—
Year 6 at Raglan C.V. Primary, 1996/7
who are, without exception, amazing.

The Legends . . .

The Sea-Harp
—which brings utter stillness to all who hear
its voice

The Sky-Egg
—which makes those who are stilled believe what
they are told

The Earthstone
—which returns to nature anything made by the
hand of man

The Sea-Harp

A cold, bright day; wind whipping sand. The Prince, walking the sea-wall, his cloak billowing, listened. Was it children, rolling and scrambling in the dunes? The sea arched and boomed, and the suck and smash of waves against the sea-wall almost smothered the second cry.

Shading his eyes, the Prince scanned the horizon. Far out, a sleek, dark head bobbed in translucent green. A seal, perhaps. But then a slender hand, white as snow, clutched at empty air and the dark head dipped beneath the waves.

The Prince plunged in, battling out from the sea-wall towards the drowning girl. She was almost dead when he reached her; the only colour in her face, small and pointed as a cat's, came from eyelids blue with cold and exhaustion. The Prince set his body between the battering stones and fragile bones, struggling to lift her onto the slippery, weed-covered wall. He succeeded, but his strength was entirely gone. Only the good fortune of a boat, passing, brought the Prince and the girl safely to shore.

She was taken to the Prince's own chamber, and women were summoned to tend her. The Prince saw her, a bedraggled flower in the richness of his bed-hangings, and his heart lurched. He knew that without her beside him, always, he was incomplete.

She opened eyes green as sea-deeps, and scrambled upright, looking frantically about her. 'The Signs! Where are the Signs?' she begged. 'Please, if you have them, give them to me.'

The Prince captured and stilled her cold hands. 'Forget them, Lady, whatever they are. Stay with me and I will give you signs—I will bring down the stars if you wish them.'

'I must have the Signs,' the sea-girl whispered. 'The Sea-King, my father, gave me permission to warn you, but without them you will not believe me. There is danger, my Lord, and I know you will not believe me.'

'What danger?' asked the Prince. 'You are safe here. What signs?'

'The Three Signs of the Sea-King,' the girl replied. 'The Sky-Egg, the Sea-Harp and the Earthstone. And the danger that faces your land will come from the sea.'

The Prince laughed. 'The sea is no danger, lady, believe me! My father, Gwyddno Garanhir, has built sea-walls so strong and tall that the wildest waves could not breach them. Lady, in twenty years not one drop of floodwater has threatened Cantre'r Gwaelod.'

'I beg you, find my Signs!' the girl pleaded, wildness in her eyes. 'Then you will believe.'

A woman brought a potion and persuaded the girl to drink. Soon, her eyelids drooped and closed. 'Dangers and signs!' the waiting-woman mocked. 'Sea-Kings! The girl is mad, my Lord!'

The Prince scowled. 'She is sick, woman!' he said, angrily.

'Oh, truly, my Lord,' the woman hastily agreed, remembering who it was that buttered her bread. 'It is a well-known fact that salt water makes folks run mad, my Lord, and likely, Sir, she will have took a chill to the marrow.'

'Stay with her,' the Prince commanded. 'See that she wants for nothing.' Reluctant to leave the girl, he laid a mattress outside the room, but exhausted, fell asleep, waking only when the chamber door thudded against his ribs.

The waiting-woman stumbled over him, rubbing daybreak into her eyes. 'Where is the Lady, my Lord?' she yawned.

The Prince came swiftly to his feet. 'In my chamber, fool. Where else?' He pushed past the bewildered woman. The chamber was empty: on the silken pillow a single dark strand of seaweed curled. The windows were tightly shut, and the room was in the tallest tower of the castle.

The Prince searched the Castle from dank cellar to bat-hung attic, but the Sea-Girl had gone. His heart despaired. He had found his life's love only to lose her in the passing of a night.

He paced the sea-wall, straining for sight of her, but the choppy waters raised false hope upon false hope, adding to his misery. He took a boat, rowing almost to the land of the giant Finn MacCool, until the night sea was dark as blood.

He was a warrior, and strong, but he wept now for his loss as he hauled the boat up on to the sand. The moon flowed pale and cold across the water, and where it touched the shore, something glinted. He stooped and lifted the shining thing, beckoning a shivering servant holding a lantern. The Prince held a sea-shell, creamy, curved, perfect; across the hollow mouth from rim to rim stretched silvery strings which, stroked, made music pure as the rivers of Cantre'r Gwaelod. Prince and servant were motionless, frozen by the exquisite sound. When he was again able to move, the Prince thought: Taliesin! Taliesin will know what this is!

Taliesin's tower, tallest in all the sixteen cities, rang with music. Sea-winds blew hollow flute-notes in the tall windows, stirring ribbons of fragile shells, and Taliesin's harp made liquid rainbows in counterpoint.

The Prince spoke softly of his love. 'She is my life,' he said, 'and she has gone. I have only this.'

Taliesin's long, clever fingers caressed the sea-harp. He stroked the strings, listening, eyes closed. Sea music swirled and coiled in the high, curved roof of the tower, shivering the great bell above. Again, the Prince was stilled by the miraculous sound.

'This is enchantment, my Prince,' Taliesin said, reluctantly surrendering the shell. What music he could make if it were his own!

'I must find her, Taliesin. I will go anywhere, travel the earth from sunrise to sunset if need be—but where shall I begin?'

Taliesin shrugged, his eyes lingering on the sea-harp. 'Perhaps Merlin can help you. He has . . . ways . . . which I lack.'

'Merlin! Of course! But where shall I find him?'

But Taliesin had lost interest, was listening to his inner music. 'He celebrates the Equinox with his King, in the northern place where the sea reflects the mountains.' His fingers stirred, and sound soared, winging like bright butterflies in the moonlit room.

The Prince paused in the doorway, frowning, remembering the banquet his father had planned. 'The Equinox, Taliesin. Tell my father where I have gone. Tell him I shall return before the celebration is done.'

The Prince rode hard. Night slipped down the hours and when he reached the royal palace in the stronghold of Gwynedd, owls glided above him, and the moon was low in the sky.

Merlin, awoken from a troubling dream concerning oak trees, doused his face and combed his tangled beard with sleep-numb fingers. A sinuous hand grasped his robe. Merlin freed himself, tenderly kissing the fingertips. 'Later, Nimue my love. There will be Time.'

12

Quickly, the Prince told Lord Merlin his story.

'The Sea-Harp!' he said. 'One of the Sea-King's Three Signs. But the Sky-Egg? The Earthstone? Where are they?'

The Prince, bone-weary, sank into a chair. 'Beneath the sunset sea, I fear. "Danger from the sea", she said. 'But Cantre'r Gwaelod is surely safe! Our defences are strong. Not even the fiercest seas could breach them.'

'And yet the Sea-King's Daughter brought the Signs,' Merlin said, thoughtfully, twisting strands of beard into grey rat-tails.

'Yes. But the Sea-King would surely not harm his own child? Merlin, she was near death! If he granted her leave to warn us, why would he prevent her bringing the Signs?'

'Your father, my Prince, has kept the Sea-King from Cantre'r Gwaelod for nigh on twenty years. The land is rich, fertile, beautiful. The Sea-King, perhaps, is hungry for what once was his.'

In Merlin's inner chamber, a great carved mirror lay on a table, wreathed in woodsmoke from the fire, reflecting the crimson wall-hangings so that it shone like a pool of dark wine. An oak-leaf spiralled from the rafters onto its surface, and testily Merlin brushed it off. He was much bothered, lately, by oaks.

At first, the Prince saw only the room's reflection, but then, in the mirror's depths he saw his father's servants preparing the Equinoctial Celebration. The surface misted and cleared again, revealing the dark interior of a small hut. A man lay, asleep or unconscious, a wine flask rolling near his outflung hand.

'The Gate-Keeper!' breathed the Prince, understanding—and believing!—at last. And then the mirror filled with wild waters and the sea-gates of Cantre'r Gwaelod, open to the rising tide.

Snatching up the Sea-Harp, the Prince mounted a fresh horse and rode, hour after hour, until his horse stumbled half-dead beneath him. The scouring wind moaned about him, and rain beat upon the curve of his back, mingling with the foam flecking the horse's heaving flanks. As night fell he reached the hills above Cantre'r Gwaelod, and looked across the Sixteen Cities. The rain had stopped and the sun stooped towards the horizon, streaking the storm-clouds crimson.

Below him, where the fertile fields and marble towers of Cantre'r Gwaelod once trapped the glow of the setting sun, tumbled a dark and terrible sea.

Taliesin's tower remained, the gleaming bell shining in the dying light, but the pitiless waters crept higher still. A shadow flickered in the bell-tower. The Prince strained his eyes to see, but it shimmered and disappeared. The tower slipped beneath the waves, and a white owl flew out and soared above it, slowly circling, ghostly in the awful light.

The Prince roared his rage, his pain, his despair at the surging waters. Blinded by tears, he took the Sea-Harp, hurling it with all his strength into the sapphire sky. It curved, beginning its downward arc, twisting, falling end over end towards the dark sea.

And from the waves came a slender hand, its fingers white as snow, and plucked the Sea-Harp from the air. The Sea-Harp and the Sea-King's Daughter disappeared beneath the waves.

Far beneath the tumbling waves the drowned bells of the Sixteen Cities of Cantre'r Gwaelod chimed deep and slow as the Moon exerted Her ancient will and turned the tide.

The Sky-Egg

. . . As the tower slipped beneath the waves, a white owl flew out and soared above it, ghostly in the awful light. The bird circled once, twice, then winged silently towards the mountains.

The journey was easier for the bird than it had been for the Prince, for the sky has no stones to stumble upon, and there was a following wind. Nevertheless, when the owl reached the High King's stronghold, it was weary, for flight was an unaccustomed thing. On the stone battlements of the great castle, the owl landed, shimmered and became, once more, Taliesin, Bard and Shapeshifter.

He was welcomed by his liege Lord the High King, and by Merlin the Necromancer, who had of course expected him, and had had servants prepare a chamber for him. After a night's sleep, Taliesin was recovered in body, but his spirit ached for Cantre'r Gwaelod and his great tower of music, and for his many musical instruments. He grieved for his friends, all of whom had drowned, but Taliesin, being immortal, did not grieve overmuch for humans: friends were easier to replace than his favourite harp, crafted from a tree sprung from the magical earth of Afallon, when the world still turned without haste. Taliesin grieved for his harp: he still had his golden voice, but a voice—even such a voice as his—without a harp was like a garden without flowers.

Merlin ignored the Bard's misery: he was still haunted by oak leaves, which collected in drifts in odd corners of his chambers, although the nearest oak was half a mile away, and his chambers were the highest, with the finest view over the narrows towards Ynys Môn. Merlin knew that

15

such omens are not granted without reason, but lately his great mirror reflected everyone else's futures but concealed his own. He munched his beard and strained his eyesight peering in his mirror, but, apart from the certainty that it contained oak-trees, his future remained hidden.

Taliesin, although always ready to recite an epic poem, or sing a song extolling the High King, knew that the borrowed harp he used only accompanied his voice, and did not embellish it, and his moods grew blacker by the day. Even the greening of summer did not lighten his mood: the bright sands and blue skies below the castle only reminded him of his lost tower of Cantre'r Gwaelod, and one day, after a disagreement with Merlin's love, the Lady Nimue, he shape-shifted into a herring gull and flew towards the cliff tops which ended so abruptly at the place where Cantre'r Gwaelod had once stretched to the sea. He wheeled downward, dropping like a stone into the sparkling sea, and as he touched the surface, shimmered himself into a sleek, silvery body with gills and fins.

He swam down, down, to where the drowned tower was, the sun dappling patterns of light on the marble walls, schools of tiny silver fish darting in through one arched window and out through another. He followed them into the tower, dark where the sun's rays could not reach, and found his instruments of hollow bone and ivory, the music-makers he had stroked, plucked and softly blown. At last he found his harp. He swam joyously in and out of the strings, stroking them with his iridescent scales, but the harp needed air to sing, and the magical instrument was silent, its intricately carved frame smothered with clinging weed. It was ruined.

Taliesin, overcome with fury, swam madly about the tower, cursing the Sea King, who had taken Cantre'r

Gwaelod and killed his harp. A sudden great pressure struck him, an undersea swell burst like a great bubble inside the tower, and Taliesin-the-fish found himself thrown high in the air by the rage of the wrathful Sea-King, who knew every thought of every creature in his domain.

Discretion being the better part of valour, Taliesin changed hastily into a cormorant, and flapped blackly to the beach, where he shape-shifted to himself again, wriggling his bones until they fitted properly. Moodily, he walked the beach, kicking sand, tossing small stones hard into the sea. Somehow he must persuade Merlin to favour him: he must get more of the magical wood to make another harp, a harp even better than the last.

Something caught his eye: a dark expanse in the cliffs, eroded by the tide's new pathways. A cave. He wandered inside the weed-hung, wet-walled blackness. The mouth was large enough for him to stand, and the cave went a way back, narrowing to a tunnel with light at the far end.

Taliesin squirmed through the narrow passage, until he was standing in a natural rock chimney which, when the tide was high and the sea-wind howled like a ravenous wolf, would send great plumes of sea-water high into the air. The day was calm, and the breeze had dried the inside of the chimney and the space around it. Taliesin looked about him. High up on a rock shelf at the point furthermost from the entrance, something glinted. It was a few seconds work to climb the cave walls, and Taliesin was soon within hands' reach of the object. He groped for it, tucked it in his jerkin and scrambled down again.

Once more on the sandy floor, he took out the object and looked at it, turning it over in his hands. It was a stone egg, the size of a goose egg and heavy. The colour dazzled; blue as the sun on a butterfly wing, or the inside of a seashell, but brighter, more iridescent than either. It shimmered, clouded, changed and shifted, and Taliesin realised that he held the second of the Sea-King's signs: the Sky-Egg.

At last, he thought, I have something to bargain with! He could force the Sea-King to return his harp. But even as the thought crossed his mind he knew it was no use. The sea had damaged his harp so completely that it would never sing again.

The journey back to the Castle was longer, because with the Sky-Egg to carry Taliesin had to travel on foot most of the way, and by cart some of the way, when a farmer kindly agreed to carry him in return for tales of the High King's deeds.

He hid the Sky-Egg in his chamber, and went about his business. And one day he found a piece of wood in the carpenter's mews which sang to him, and although it would not, could not, ever be as fine as the Afallon harp, it would be a good harp when he had given it voice and made it his own.

He might have forgotten the Sky-Egg if Merlin had not wandered distractedly into his chamber one day to watch him work on the harp-frame. Dry oak leaves rustled and whispered in his hair and clung to his robes, and he tugged fretfully at his beard, afraid that his powers were deserting him, for he was still unable to see his own future, and cared nothing for anyone else's. He gazed absent-mindedly out of the chamber window, listening to Taliesin's soft, contented humming, and the steady whisper of the knife freeing leaves and roses from the wood. Turning from the window, he saw the Sky-Egg, and knew at once what it was.

'How did you come by this?' he asked, and Taliesin explained.

18

Merlin frowned. 'It is not wise to keep something that belongs to one of the Oldest Ones,' he warned. 'The Sea-King will seek it, and we may all suffer.'

Taliesin laughed bitterly. 'The Sea-King stole my harp,' he said. 'The Sea-Egg is mine. He shall not have it. What can he do? After all is said, his kingdom is beneath the waves.'

Merlin looked sternly at him. 'You, who saw the end of Cantre'r Gwaelod, can ask that question? Come, Taliesin. The Autumn Equinox is near, with its high tide. Even mountains have been known to wash to the sea.'

Taliesin scowled. 'I tell you I will keep it. I shall not give it back. It is mine.'

Merlin, shaking his head, returned to his chamber and his mirror. Perhaps hen-bane and sea-pink; maybe lizards instead of frogs—there must be some way to discover his future . . .

But the Sea King had heard, and knew Taliesin had his Sky-Egg, and he wanted it back. Taliesin soon realised that he was in danger: he could no longer take pleasure in walking the shore. Mighty waves appeared from nowhere to engulf him, and once, he saved himself only by climbing the cliffs. As he stood looking out to sea, a tremendous wind hurled itself at his back, and only by throwing himself flat on his face was he able to prevent being flung on the rocks below. Worst of all, he dived one day into a sea-pool, came up spluttering, shaking his hair back from his face, dashing water from his eyes—and was face to face with a monstrous sea-serpent with teeth like daggers and a hungry look. That time he survived only by disguising himself as a sea-anemone until the serpent gave up the hunt.

The Sea-King wanted his Sky-Egg.

Autumn and the high tides were coming, and so Taliesin, increasingly worried, consulted Merlin, who did not tell Taliesin that he had told him so. He stroked his beard and consulted several books, brushing oak-leaves from the covers and between the pages.

'You do not wish to return the Egg?' he asked slyly, knowing Taliesin's pride would not allow him to do so.

'Never!' said Taliesin. 'I would rather die.'

'Unfortunately,' Merlin replied drily, 'it may come to that.'

'Merlin, there must be something I can do?'

The Necromancer, on tiptoe, reached down a huge book from a high shelf and blew off the oak-leaf tangled cobwebs. He pored over it. 'The only way to defeat the power of the Sea King,' he said at last, 'according, that is, to Cartinomanciportalus the Lesser whose major work this is,' he continued learnedly, showing off, 'is to bury the object in another Eternal Oldness.'

Taliesin frowned, trying to understand. 'Eternal Oldness—?' (He was a musician, and had been single-minded in his studies).

'Earth, Sea and Sky,' Merlin said impatiently.

Taliesin thought. 'I cannot hide the Sky-Egg in water,' he said, 'for the Sea-King has dominion over all the seas, and all rivers run to the sea. And the Sky is the Egg's own element and so . . .'

'You must bury it in the earth,' Merlin said, then added quickly '—but it should be buried a long, long way from here—perhaps a hundred leagues. Or more !'

Taliesin looked bewildered. 'But why?'

'Cartinomanciportalus the Lesser is—ah—somewhat out of date,' Merlin said. 'To bury it too close to the High

King's summer palace would be unwise. Considering all the various considerations, that is.'

And so, next day, carrying the Sky-Egg carefully wrapped in linen and soft hides, Taliesin rode out from the High King's castle. He rode for a day and a half, carefully avoiding any place where the sea met the land, and crossing rivers only at low tide and well away from tidal estuaries, until he came to a small village named after Ceredig, an ancient tribe steeped in magical ways. Late that night, by the light of a wondrous moon, he buried the Sky Egg, still wrapped in its linen and hide, at the cross-roads of the village, which would one day become a bustling market-town. The cross-roads, up on a small hill, pointed North to the mountains, South to the great fortress on the Taf many miles distant, East to the blue hills of Middle Wales—and West to the sea. And Taliesin smiled as he dug, for the Sea-King's domain was only a small distance away, and had the Sea-King looked in Taliesin's direction, he would have seen his Sign hidden away— perhaps forever—under the dark brown earth of Cymru.

The Earthstone

Taliesin mounted his horse, and began the long journey back. Returning, it was not necessary to avoid the cliffs and estuaries, for he no longer carried anything which the Sea-King desired. He paused at the place where Cantre'r Gwaelod had been, and gazed at the shore far below.

When the storms had subsided, the new coast line knew the ebb and flow of tides, and sea-eroded cliffs revealed ancient boulders, bones of strange and mighty beasts, and a narrow, sandy shore. Taliesin's horse lowered its head to crop the coarse, salty turf. Far below, his body made squat by the height of the cliffs, a man moved slowly, stopping here and there. Taliesin watched him for a while: he was collecting rocks, it seemed, and putting them into a basket strapped to his back.

A transparent fingernail moon rose over the sea, and Taliesin knew that he had to make camp for the night, for he had no hope of reaching the stronghold before dark, and he was tired. Pulling up his reluctant horse's head, Taliesin rode away from the clifftop, looking for a sheltered place to sleep. A little way back, in a stand of birch trees, he found a pile of scattered stones: the copse would provide shelter from the sea-winds. He turned his horse loose to graze, constructed a fire-circle and built a fire. He ate a supper of bread and cold meat, listening to flaming wood spit and crack, watching sparks fly upward, and drowsily wondered if he could turn such night sounds into harp-music. So intent was he on the music of nightingale, owl-hoot and crackling fire that he did not hear the stealthy footsteps creeping up behind him, and failed to sense the presence of the intruder until a twig cracked underfoot. But by then it was too late: there was a knife pricking at his throat, and a rough hand entangled in his hair.

'Do not struggle,' a gruff voice said. 'You trespass in my home. This land is mine.'

Taliesin, knowing that immortals need not fear knives, pushed at the hand holding the weapon. 'Your home? Your land? This is the border of Cantre'r Gwaelod. If it belongs to anyone it belongs to the son of Gwyddno Garanhir. What right have you to call it yours?'

Startled by Taliesin's boldness, the man lowered the knife, but did not let go of Taliesin's hair until he had relieved him of the small dagger he carried in his belt. Then, both knives projecting like thorns, and watchful for sudden movement, the man moved to the other side of the fire, allowing Taliesin to sit up.

'This land is no man's, I say. And by the ancient tradition of Tŷ Un Nos, I claim it.'

Taliesin laughed. 'In years to come that Law will be written down, I dare say, by some great King, but all men know that the house must be built, and a fire kindled in the hearth, between sunset and sunrise of one day. You have a heap of stones, man—but it is nearer sunrise than sunset and the fire is mine. What do they call you, house-builder?'

The man hung his head. 'I am Eifion Gwyn. For my hair, Sir, which is white. And had it not already been white, this place would surely have made it so.'

Taliesin, sensing the bones of a story, leaned forward, the firelight flickering red on his face. 'What do you mean?'

Eifion Gwyn pursed his lips. 'Two days I laboured, between sunrise and sunset, carrying stones one by one from the shore, and damned heavy they was, my Lord, beggin' your pardon. Two times in two nights I built four

23

walls and a hearthstone for a fire, and twice I cut branches for a roof. Twice I lit fires in the hearth and twice I spread straw to sleep on beside 'em. And after carrying them stones up from the shore, and a-buildin' my house, I can tell you, your Greatness, I slept sound as a pig in a sty, no matter it was bright day.'

'And?' prompted Taliesin.

'Twice, my Lord,' the man said, glumly, 'two times I have woke and found only this one wall, and that scattered to the four winds. At first I thought someone were playing a trick on me, hiding my house. But today—for the third time, mind—I began collecting stones to build again, tonight, and I realised that every stone I found had been returned to the exact place I'd took 'em from! Only this one little pile remains, and that were here afore I started. The Tylwyth Teg must've took 'em, Sir, not nothin' from this world.'

Taliesin scowled. 'Why should the Other World bother you? Who are you*? Nobody!'*

'Exackly, Sir,' agreed Eifion Gwyn humbly. 'There is not many lower than what I am. But this bit of land, nobody owns, nobody farms. It's just the place for a Tŷ Un Nos. I thought I would try to better myself. But no man can build here.'

Taliesin loved a challenge. 'Tomorrow, when it is light, I will look at this wall.' Then he rolled himself in his blanket and fell asleep.

Eifion Gwyn was not happy to have Taliesin share his space. Although he lay down on the other side of the fire, and closed his eyes, he clutched both knives firmly, and slept poorly. But Taliesin, immortal and unafraid, slept soundly in the warmth of the crackling fire.

Dawn slid sideways between the trees of the grove, waking the two men. When they had eaten and it was fully

24

light, Taliesin inspected the small heap of stones. At first, he saw nothing strange: just flat, smooth stones. Some of the stones were blackened with smoke from the fires that Eifion Gwyn had built on his disappearing hearthstones, but Taliesin could see nothing out of the ordinary. And then he touched one, and leapt back as if he had been burned.

'What is it, my Lord?' Eifion cried. Taliesin's entire arm was numb, and the nerves of elbow and wrist tingled. He knew then that the wall was magical.

'Touch the stones, Eifion!' he commanded.

'Well, now, begging your pardon, Sir,' Eifion Gwyn said, politely, 'but if them stones attacked a Lordship like yourself, what hope is there for such as me? As you rightly said, Sir, I am nobody, and the stones will have even less respeck for me.'

'You are the nobody who built the wall, Eifion Gwyn,' Taliesin said. 'The stones should not harm you.'

'Should not and will not is two different things, my Lord,' Eifion grumbled, but he closed his eyes, gritted his teeth, and gingerly touched the stones. Nothing happened.

Taliesin smiled. There was certainly magic here. Something in the heap of stones had reacted to his own powers. But what?

It was difficult to persuade Eifion Gwyn to move the stones, but eventually he agreed. Taliesin peered at each one as Eifion lifted it, and touched one or two, but away from the heap, they were just ordinary stone. And then, towards the bottom of the pile, Eifion Gwyn removed a stone which Taliesin knew, immediately, was the one he sought. It was oval, not round, and in the centre was a perfectly round hole. Wedged in the hole, so that it could be turned, but not removed, was an irregularly shaped piece of rock, containing shiny particles that glistened in the morning sun.

'Where did you get this?' Taliesin asked. 'From the shore, I know, but where? Surely it was not lying exposed?'

Eifion Gwyn shook his head. 'No, Sir. This partic'lar stone, as I recall, was well hid. There is a cave above the tide-line, where the recent high seas washed the cliff away. In the rock was the bones of some great beast—mayhap a dragon, Sir, who knows? This partic'lar stone was in the rib-cage of the skellington, stuck fast in the wall of the cave. Took me an age, Sir, I can tell you, but I got it out in the end. I'd took a fancy to it, you see, Sir.'

Taliesin knew that here was the third of the Sea-King's Signs: the Earthstone.

He smiled. 'Eifion Gwyn,' he said graciously, 'I shall take this stone.'

Eifion Gwyn considered, eying Taliesin suspiciously. 'If this stone is valuable, Sir, then perhaps I should keep it and sell it. It is my stone. That much is certain an' sure, Sir, for it don't attack me, do it? Beggin' your pardon for saying so, Sir.'

'It is not valuable,' Taliesin said. 'But it is powerful magic. Who knows, Eifion Gwyn, it could be dangerous. It might turn on you one night, and dismantle you, bone from bone, sinew from sinew, until your blood runs like wine on the earth.'

Hastily, Eifion laid the stone on the ground. 'Take it, Sir. When it is gone, then will I be able to build my house?'

'Once the Earthstone is gone your house can be built, Eifion Gwyn'. Taliesin bent and touched the stone, carefully. His fingertips tingled, but away from Eifion's wall the Earthstone's power was harnessed. 'I shall take this to Merlin,' he said. 'Merlin will know how to keep it safely.'

Eifion gaped. 'You know the Great Merlin?' he asked. 'Who are you, Sir?'

The bard smiled, his vanity touched. 'I am Taliesin, Music-Maker, once Bard to Elffin, to Gwyddno Garanhir, and now Great Bard to the High King himself.'

Eifion was suitably awed. 'Will you put me in a song, Lord Taliesin?' he asked hopefully. 'Seems like I ought to get put in a song, Sir. Not many nobodies finds magic stones.'

Taliesin saddled his horse. 'Who knows, Eifion Gwyn of the White Hair. When the bards come to your hearth, in the house that you will build, listen closely. Lesser bards hear my songs. All imitate them,' he finished, smugly, and rode away.

At the top of the hill he looked back. Eifion Gwyn, a small, persistent ant, was rebuilding his wall.

Merlin was sweeping rustling heaps of oak-leaves from his chamber when Taliesin returned. Nimue planned a picnic in the forest, and Merlin had a strange feeling that his problems were near solution. Therefore he had little time for Taliesin, although he was enchanted to have the last of the Sea-King's Signs, and turned it over and over in his hands, sunlight sparkling on the glistening flecks in the Earthstone's heart.

'May I keep this Sign?' Taliesin asked plaintively. 'The Sea-Harp has been returned to the sea, the Sky-Egg is safely hidden—why should I not keep this one last Sign?'

Merlin shrugged, his mind on Nimue. 'As you wish,' he said carelessly. 'But you will never spend another night under a roof. This is the Earthstone, Taliesin. It takes back everything that man takes from the natural world. Wooden walls become trees again, stones return to the earth—and harps, Taliesin, even beautifully carved and lovingly strung ones, also return to source. If you value your livelihood, you will hide the Earthstone as well as you hid the Sky Egg.'

Taliesin sighed. 'Am I never to keep any of the magical things that come my way?' he complained. 'My Afallon harp, the Sea-Harp, the Sky-Egg all gone. And now, the Earthstone.' A thought occurred to him. 'But how can I hide it? If I throw it in the sea the Sea King will have it. If I throw it in a river it will wash to the sea, and if I bury it, nothing will stand one stone on another for miles around. What can I do with it, Merlin? Find an eagle's nest in the mountains and leave it there?'

Merlin shook his head, dislodging a shower of oak leaves and an acorn or two from his beard. 'You must find the source of a river, where a clear spring bubbles from bare rock, and you must put the Earthstone in an iron box and place it where the water gushes. Iron, as you well know, will defeat Earth Magic.'

So Taliesin took the Earthstone and placed it in an iron box. He traced the river which ran into the hills of Middle Wales until he found the cleft in the mountains far away from the Great King's stronghold. Crystal water, icy cold, bubbled and sang from the bare rock, and here Taliesin laid the box, so that clear water sluiced over it. In years to come the box turned first green with waterweed, and then dark, rusty brown, transformed by the rushing water so that it became indistinguishable from the rocks among which it was hidden.

CHAPTER ONE

First, I blamed my Dad. Then I blamed my Mom. Then I got bored with sulking and slamming doors and put all the blame firmly on Mr Takahashi.

Mr Takahashi is my Dad's boss: he is OK, I guess, and kinda nice when you meet him. But after what he's done to me, I won't forgive him if I live to be a hundred and ten. He has RUINED my LIFE.

It might not seem so awful to you, I guess, but it sure is to me! I'd just gotten a try-out for cheerleader, I was on the swimming team, I was almost-but-not-quite going steady with Kurt Bonadetti and what happens? Total *tragedy*, that's what. Mr Takahashi sends my Dad—and my Mom, and my brother Jake and me—to the other end of the *planet*, for gosh sake! I asked my Dad 'Why us?', but he said 'Why not?' and that was that. 'It'll be a great opportunity for you kids to see something of the world,' he said. 'So lighten up, sweetheart, and try to be reasonable.'

But I didn't *want* to lighten up and be reasonable, I wanted to be real teed off, and let my Dad know that I didn't wanna be uprooted from my home and my friends and sent to the back end of nowhere.

I guess if I was fair about it (which I most certainly did not intend to be), it was kind of obvious why us. Mr Takahashi wants to open a Takahashi Electronics factory in Wales, England, and so the obvious person to send is my Dad, David Rhys Morgan. Dad is descended from a Welshman who settled in Pennsylvania about fifteen minutes, if you believe my Dad, after the Pilgrim Fathers hit Plymouth Rock!

My Dad got real excited about going, and my Mom got

caught up in *his* excitement so it got kind of difficult to be mega-sulky around them, 'cos they just didn't notice! Also, I started to feel left out, which I do not like one bit, and also, Jake was being a real zit. Sheesh!—he's such a creep, Jake! He don't care where he is so long as he's got his Walkman and his dumb-A.. computer games. Also, he thought that England being kind of a backward country, school would be a whole lot easier. Anyway, anything I really, totally, majorly do *not* want to do, you can bet your last banana Jake will say he does, just to tick me off. Anyhow, I couldn't go on being a jerk, I guess—at least, not the only jerk in the family. So, rather than be odd guy out, I stopped being a drag—but man, did I ever moan to my best friend Kymmburleigh.

I know! Just *awful* isn't it? But it's her Mom and Dad's fault, not hers. Kym has majorly, major, problems with her folks: they are lousy ones for a great kid like Kym to have. They are real fat, for a start, and her Mom wears weird clothes, and their house is called 'BUDLOUKYM' because her Dad is Bud, her Mom is Louelle, and they tagged poor Kym on the end. Kym wishes she had neat parents like my Mom and Dad. She just *begs* her folks not to go to P.T.A. meetings and the Dads' and Daughters' Proms, stuff like that, she's so embarrassed by them. I kind of agree with her, I have to, I'm her best friend, but actually, I guess they're OK, no matter how they look and act. If they don't have good taste they're still ncie enough, y'know?

At least I got the right reaction from Kym when I told her. 'Omigosh, Kym,' I said 'the pits! The most majorly, majorly, major worst! My Dad's got to go work in England, and Mom and me and Jake gotta go with him.'

Kym opened her eyes and mouth real wide, clutched her

chest, like this, closed her eyes and mouth again and moaned through her teeth, 'Nnnnnnnngh!'

'Omigosh, Cat!' she groaned, 'I cannot BEAR IT! You cannot GO. You're my best friend, ever. I'll die if you go, I'll just die, I know I will!' Her eyes filled up with tears and rolled down her cheeks. I hugged her.

'Yeah,' I said, gloomily. 'It's a bummer, ain't it?'

It got even more of a bummer. Miss Exeter in the eighth grade organised a 'Catrin is leaving' shower. That's not the whole class standing under running water in the locker rooms, like it sounds, but a party where everybody brings a gift, and hugs you, and all the girls cry a whole lot. I had a real great time, I cried and cried until my eyes were all red and swollen up. I had a great time, that is, right up to when Kym told me she'd seen Kurt Bonadetti kissing Sammi-Su Manners in back of the sports hall! That jerk didn't even wait until after I'd gone. It sure spoiled my party, I can tell you. But I guess it rounded off leaving home OK because it meant there was at least ONE person I wouldn't miss!

We flew out of Kennedy on a wonderful, sunshiny June day. I bawled so long and hard at leaving America and all my friends that I missed the take-off AND most of the in-flight movie, which was also a majorly major bummer, because Keanu Reeves was in it. Also I got to sit next to Jake, who played electronic games the whole way, never mind I told him the electronics might interfere with the flight computer and make the plane crash into the sea, killing us all. Also he had his headphones on and Guns 'N Roses squeaking but not loud enough to hear good, and he wouldn't talk at all, so I was all alone with my miseries because Mom and Dad were a couple or three rows back. It would have been totally boring if it hadn't been for a little kid who played hide-and-go-seek all over the plane and seriously annoyed all the grownups!

When we finally arrived, I have to be real honest: I was NOT IMPRESSED by London. Not even driving past the Houses of Parliament and Big Ben. Mainly, London, England just seemed busy and dirty and full, like any other big city, and it rained a whole lot, so we had to splash through puddles to get to our hotel.

When we got into the Grand Imperial Duchess Hotel the doorman held a big umbrella over my Mom's head, just like in the movies, and then we went up in the elevator to our suite, which was real elegant. A room for Mom and Dad, a little sitting room with a TV in between, and little rooms each for Jake and me. When we'd unpacked, I showered and changed and got ready to go down to dinner (Jake just changed—he doesn't like hot water and soap much, but I guess nine year old boys are like that). We were idly flipping through the TV channels waiting for Mom and Dad. Then we discovered the TV was faulty, I could only find four channels plus the video channel.

I hollered 'Dad! Could I call reception and get a guy up to change this set? I can't find the cartoon channel, or the movie channel, or . . .'

Dad laughed, real hard. 'That's all there is, honey!' he called. 'You're in England now. They have cable TV in some places, I think, but not too many. I guess not where we're going—but you can listen to whole programmes in the Welsh language! Won't that be *great*?'

The look of horror on Jake's face almost made up for my own shock! What were we gonna do for entertainment, for petesake? Knitting?

Dad, coming out of the bedroom and seeing our faces, grinned. 'Don't worry, you guys. You'll have plenty to do—and you'll make friends real fast just as soon as you start school.'

32

Mom came out of the bedroom and turned her back for Dad to pull the zipper on her dress. He kissed her cheek when he was done and Jake made a barfing sound and said 'Sheesh, knock it off, you guys.' He hates it when they get mushy.

Dad put his arms round Mom from behind. They made a good picture, you know? Dad is very tall and red-haired, and Mom is small and dark and green-eyed, so I get my auburn hair from my Dad, and my green eyes from my Mom. It gives me a real good feeling to see them together. When I was a little kid, I used to worry a whole lot, because scads of my friends back home have parents who are divorced, and remarried, sometimes a couple or more times, and they thought it was kind of weird that my Mom and Dad were still together after *centuries*. Then I realised they were actually kinda envious of me and Jake! Anyway, there they were, grinning at us, being happy.

That was when I started to feel better. I had an opportunity to get to know a whole new country, and my Mom, Dad, Jake and me were all together, so nothing could be too awful, could it? I guessed I'd survive the next couple of years.

Then we went down to dinner in this real smart Hotel and I almost changed my mind. The restaurant was full of waiters in penguin suits, and there were huge crystal chandeliers dangling above us, and I felt kinda grown up when the waiter pulled out my chair for me to sit down, and shook out my napkin. He tried to do the same for Jake, but Jake wasn't having any of *that* stuff, he just snatched it back, scowling. I sipped some fizzy mineral water from a stemmed glass, and pretended it was champagne, and sat back and really started to enjoy myself, you know?

And THEN we had the worst meal I have EVER eaten

33

in MY WHOLE LIFE! First off, I wanted a burger and fries.

Dad said, 'No, honey, they don't do that stuff here. We're in England now, and we're going to eat a real English roast dinner. We're gonna eat the roast beef of Old England! No more junk food!'

So first we had soup, and then omigosh, if you've ever eaten a warm, soggy, Kentucky Fried chicken *carton*, that's what the roast beef was like. They served a kind of puffy, hollow thing with it that tasted of nothing.

'Real Yorkshire Pudding,' Dad said, happily, chomping. It was awful! The Yorkshires could keep it. Even Jake, who will eat most anything, didn't finish up. And my Dad called *burgers* junk food! At least we had ice-cream for dessert, but they didn't have many flavours—no pecan dash or honey-butter-toffee, or cookies-and-cream, or raisin and peanut butter, or mint choc chip. Just boring old vanilla and strawberry. Not even chocolate, for gosh sake!

Jet lag caught up with us next day and we kept falling asleep, so stayed around the hotel and dozed, and the day after that we got a car and a driver, thanks to Mr Takahashi, and saw London: the Tower, Hampton Court, the Houses of Parliament, Big Ben and all until I felt like I had history running out my ears! England is all so OLD! It makes our couple of hundred years kind of pathetic when you think England has real history going way, way back, our driver Stan said—to before ten-sixty-six. Stan told us about something that happened back then, something to do with some guy called Norman, but he talked so weird I couldn't understand half he said.

Dad was real impressed, and kept saying 'Wow!' and 'Gosh, honey!' and 'Will you look at that!' and 'I just HAVE to photograph THAT!' until even Stan, who was getting paid for driving us around, was getting kinda teed off with finding places to park so Dad could take photographs.

We didn't risk dinner at the hotel that night—we went out and FOUND A MACDONALD'S! I got awful homesick, going under the golden arch, and inside it looked exactly like our MacDonalds back home. When our food arrived, and Jake and me had great big grins, then Dad told us we had to stop calling it 'England'.

'You see, guys, we're in England *now*,' he explained, 'but our new home is in Wales, and Wales is a whole separate, different country, and you've got to remember that. This whole little island is called "Great Britain", and it's made up of England, and Scotland, and Ireland, and Wales. And the English live in England, and the Scots live in Scotland, and the Irish live in Ireland, and—'

'And the Welsh live in Russia,' Jake said, wearily. 'Yeah, sure, Dad.'

I said 'Yes, Dad,' and 'No, Dad,' but I wasn't really paying too much attention, because at the time I had my teeth wrapped around a real juicy Big Mac and fries, and dill pickle, and cheese, and tomato ketchup, and salad, and there was a bright picture of Ronnie MacD. across the room, looking at me, and it kind of felt like it was a link with home.

I may have started to feel a bit better about having to come to England—sorry, Dad, Great Britain—but boy, was I homesick! I missed all my buddies back home, and when we got back to the hotel that night I sat down at the desk in my room and wrote Kym, licking tears off my face as they dripped off my nose so they wouldn't make soggy patches on the Grand Imperial Duchess Hotel's real elegant headed notepaper. We'd agreed before I left that we'd each write a bit of a letter each day, and save it up until we had a whole week's worth, and then mail it, so we could still be best friends even though we were thousands of miles apart. I brushed my teeth every night with the Stars and Bars toothbrush she'd given me at my farewell shower, and wore my Mickey Mouse shower cap (with ears) I'd gotten at Disneyland, and wore my 'I ♥ America' baseball cap all day, and felt kinda closer to home.

On Friday, we left London, England, picked up Dad's company car from Takahashi UK headquarters, and drove down to Pontpentre-dŵr, Wales, which would be our home for at least the next three years. At least Dad was excited, once he got used to driving on the wrong side of the road, and to how fast all the other cars went. We practised saying 'Pontpentre-dŵr', which Dad had already learned how to pronounce. Jake managed it OK, but I kept getting it wrong and dribbling down my T-shirt a whole lot. I hoped there were some normal place names, like 'Texas' and 'New York' and 'Baton Rouge', because 'Pontpentre-dŵr' didn't make too much sense to me, and if I got myself lost, how would I ask my way home when I couldn't even *say* the darn place?

Dad grinned at me in the rear view mirror. 'Did you guys know there's a place back home called Bryn Mawr? he asked. 'That's Welsh, and there's a real expensive girls' college there. And that place was started up by some Welsh people.'

I yawned. 'You don't say, Dad!' I said sleepily, the rainy grey highway to Wales beginning to bore me.

'It's a whole new world out there, kids!' he said. 'New places, new language, new school, new friends! What an opportunity!'

'Yeah, Dad,' I said, and fell asleep

36

CHAPTER TWO

When I woke up, we were away from London, but everything still seemed real dirty and was full of factories and gas stations and stuff. My heart crept right down into my sneakers. England—sorry, Dad, Britain—looked ugly, and cramped, and filthy, and the thought of spending *years* there was just *gross*. There were greenish bits, and some small, untidy towns, but mostly it was just two or three lane freeways, with all the other automobiles being driven too fast on *totally* the wrong side of the road!

Then Dad took the turn-off to Gloucester. He said it would be quicker to get into Wales across the Severn Bridge, but he wanted us to see Wales first from its best side. It got kind of interesting then, with little twisty roads, and miles of green fields, and trees, stuff like that, and even some real thatched cottages! Y'know, it's real odd. I knew what English thatched cottages looked like, but seeing a real live one, I was, like, totally blown away! They REALLY DO have straw roofs. Far out!

The road twisty-turned up and down hills, and then we were driving beside a broad brown river. The rain stopped, the sun came out and a rainbow arched into a blue sky scattered with big white clouds like heaps of whipped cream. The river glinted in the sun, and the raindrops on the windscreen sparkled.

The land each side of the river was pasture, with real cows and sheep, then it became hills looking like a pink boucle sweater I once had, only a deep, dark, rich green, not pink. Millions of trees, stretching forever, with kind of a mysterious, waiting-for-something-to-happen look about them. And this was beside a freeway! There was even a

37

pair of swans on the river, and before I'd had time to gasp about *that*, there was this sign, with a big, red dragon on it, and the words

Croeso i Gymru

Then my Dad went 'Yeee-haaar!' and punched the air, laughing like an idiot. Mom grinned right back and slugged him real hard on the arm, and said 'Hey, honey, you're home!'

Dad turned round in the driving seat to grin at Jake and me, and he looked so happy I couldn't help smiling back, even though I didn't feel like Wales was *anything* to do with *me*. It was just a place we were going to live for a while.

A couple of miles further on, we went past our first Welsh town, Monmouth, where Dad said some Henry or other had been born. Then he started quoting Shakespeare at us, so Jake put his headphones on again. He took them off again when we got to a place called Raglan, because up on the hill right beside the freeway was a real castle! Kind of broken up in places, but a real Castle. Jake got majorly excited and said, 'Wow! That's real neat, Dad. Can we stop off and explore? Please Dad?', but Dad said we didn't have time.

'We'll do it some other time, I promise,' he said. 'Wales is full of castles, Jake—I doubt we'll get to see them all even if we are staying three years!'

Jake kept looking back through the rear window until it was gone. 'If we had a castle like that back home,' he said, thoughtfully, 'we'd have built it up again. The English are real dumb, letting it fall down.'

Mom and me chorused 'Welsh!!' and Dad laughed. 'The broken down bits are history, too, Jake.'

'It'd look a whole lot better if they put it back together, Dad. People'd get real wet in a castle with no roof,' Jake insisted.

Next, we went through a place called Abergavenny, which had a smaller castle, and then into some mountains called Beacons, which swooped all round us like great green giants, nowhere near as big as the Rockies, but kind of exciting anyway, because they were real dark and brooding. Then I fell asleep again.

When I woke up it was close to dark, and we were driving into a tiny yard with one or two cars already parked in it.

I stretched, yawning. 'Where . . .?' I mumbled.

'Aberaeron,' Dad said, 'in Ceredigion. Or Cardigan if you prefer. I decided we'd stop off here and go on to the house in the morning. I want you guys to see it in daylight.'

That was just fine by me: all I wanted was food and bed. I stumbled sleepily out of the car and almost flash-froze, like a fish finger! At the end of the little yard was a little wall, and beyond that was a little harbour, and beyond the little harbour was the great, big open sea, and there was a wind coming off that sea that felt like it was armed to the teeth with razors!

'Sheesh, Dad!' I said, hugging myself 'If this is summer, what the heck is winter gonna be like?' The sea smelled kind of salty and good, though.

Inside the creaky little hotel (kinda different to the Royal Imperial etcetera!) doors opened off and corridors bent around, and the floor planks went up and down like a fun-house at the fair. The sound of clinking glasses, laughter and voices talking a strange language drifted out from the bar, along with a nice-nasty smell of beer and cigarette smoke. Dad signed the register and the bartender carried our cases up the narrow staircase.

Then Dad got talking to this guy—this *perfect stranger*—telling him all about us. I was SO EMBARRASSED! Sure he was interested. Not! I mean, he didn't know us from a hole in the wall! The guy was nodding and smiling, and saying 'Well, goodness me,' stuff like that, polite-type words. He wasn't interested in what Dad was saying and was just being nice, I guess.

Then he opened up the door of a room, took the cases in, put them down, and turned and shook my Dad's hand. I was kind of surprised, because in the States when a guy carries your bags upstairs, he sticks his hand out for a tip, not a shake!

He had a dark face, shadowed with beard, but he was smiling like he really meant it, real friendly.

'Welcome home, Cymro,' he said. '*Croeso*!'

And my Dad all but burst out crying! Jake and me looked sidelong at each other and Jake pulled his barfing face. My Dad cleared his throat and frowned, kinda getting control of himself.

'What'd he say, Dad?' I asked, as soon as the man had shown Jake and me our rooms and gone downstairs.

'Welcome home, son of Wales,' my Dad translated, grinning proudly from ear to ear. 'What a welcome, honey!'

This was one seriously weird place!

I shook my head pityingly and looked at Jake. Son of Wales my left eyeball! Son of Pittsburgh, Pennsylvania more like! Then my Mom and Dad got to hugging each other, then they hugged us. Parents can be SOOOO embarrrrassing!

'Can we go eat, please?' I said. 'I'm starved.'

I lay awake most of the night. It was majorly awful! Kinda loudly quiet, y'know? There was no traffic noise, honking horns, police sirens, stuff like that—just the sound of the sea crashing around outside my window, and when I finally dropped off this real tinny town hall clock in the square outside the hotel said 'BINGGGG', loudly, and woke me up again. So next morning my eyes were red and gritty, I was *not* in a good humour, and even the huge bacon and egg breakfast didn't cheer me up any.

We said goodbye to the nice guy and his wife, and then we got in the car again and headed for Pontpentre-dŵr, with Dad still trying to teach me to say it right all the way there. I was still getting it wrong, and Mom, Dad and Jake were all laughing at me. Then we arrived.

We turned off the main road (road, ha! One lane, in each direction, and *still* everyone drove real fast) on to a side road with only room for ONE car in the middle. Mom was navigating, the map open against the windscreen, and Dad drove, and I sat in back and worried about what would happen if another car decided *it* wanted to use the road in the opposite direction. Smash-up city, folks, that's what! We drove across a little hump-backed bridge, followed the river along a bit more, and then, we stopped.

'Here we are,' Dad said, his voice full of satisfaction.

'What! Here?' Mom and I said, together. We were *miles* from *anywhere*! It was like, totally unbelievable! Like civilisation hadn't been *invented* yet! I'd never even *dreamed* we wouldn't be at least in some kind of *town*!

'Yup,' Dad said, opening the car door. 'Welcome to the Toll House.'

'Troll House?' Mom asked weakly, looking as if she wanted to stay where she was and go back home right then. 'They have trolls in Wales?'

41

Dad laughed. 'No, honey! Not Troll house, Toll House. A genuine, eighteenth-century Toll House right next to a genuine seventeenth-century Toll Bridge,' Dad said proudly. 'I knew you'd love it just the minute I first saw it. We're right alongside the river, and just over there is the sea, so you kids have your very own seashore to play on.' He waved his arm towards the oddest clump of trees I'd seen in my whole life, all bent over, leaning in the same direction, the leaves and branches huddled together as if they were trying to escape from something. Then I got out of the car and realised what: the wind. It pushed me back two yards before I stopped staggering! I got this vision of me, going home in three years time looking just like the trees, permanently bent by the wind like the Hunchback of Notre Dame. The house was the squarest house I'd ever seen, with four arched windows, two upstairs and two down, each side of a heavy wooden door in a stone archway. It looked like Dracula's house in the movies, only without the fog. On the left, outside, stone steps teetered up to the first floor and another door, an extension with a third door and a small, square window clutched the right side of the house. Another lean-to, smaller still, leaned against the side of this, at right-angles, like the third little pig in the story. The house was crowned by a stern-looking, squarely-pointed roof covered in black slates, and the windows were kinda *glaring at us*. Mom said, in a very, very, very small voice 'Uh. Does it have central heating, honey?'

'Ha!' Dad said, 'Sure does! A genuine 18th-century house, with genuine twentieth-century heating. Also real open fires like you always wanted back home and couldn't have because of the zoning laws.'

'Shower?' she asked, hopefully.

Dad nodded, proudly. 'Whole thing, honey. Just like back home.'

Mom grinned a brave grin. 'Hot showers and open fires, huh. Sounds just like Dickens.'

Dad hugged her. 'Dickens didn't have showers, sweetheart, but otherwise, yeah. Just like Dickens.'

'Real pneumonia, too,' I said, freezing to death in the icy wind. '*Just* like Dickens'. But neither of them heard me.

Jake shrugged, still plugged into his Walkman, and pulled his jacket collar up around his ears. Mom and me looked at each other. The house looked so darn square, and stern, and dark.

Dad opened the creaky iron gate and led the way up the red-tiled pathway to the front door. He lifted a flowerpot by an iron bar thing and found a huge black iron key.

Mom, Jake and me stood bunched together for warmth like the Babes in the Wood. Dad wrestled with the key and got the door open, and we trooped inside. Right then, it wouldn't have surprised me to find a witch inside. It was colder inside than outside. The front door opened directly into a large room, furnished with the oddest collection of furniture I'd ever seen, like it had been picked up at the City Dump! Nothing matched anything else. My Mom's face! I guess she was remembering our big, airy house, with the cream loungers and tan carpets, and the big windows . . .

A half-dozen flowery patterned chairs, all with dips in the middle as if they'd been sat on forever by someone real fat, were standing around, and a big black wooden seat thing stood alongside the fireplace. The tiled floor was scrappily covered by some multi-coloured, untidy looking rugs. The biggest thing in the room was a huge black open-

43

fronted cupboard lurking against the wall, so big that I felt
that if I looked at it wrong, it might jump on me, and
squash me like a bug. Its shelves and hooks were crammed
with blue and white china which, when I got close enough
to look, was covered in cracks, like crazy paving. We'd
probably all die of ptomaine poisoning, if we didn't die of
cold first. The house smelled peppery, and faintly of
lavender polish.

'Real, hooked rag rugs!' Dad said proudly, pointing at
the ugly things on the floor.

'And a genuine Welsh dresser;' he opened a cupboard in
the wall '—and . . .'

There was a bed inside! I ask you, a *bed* inside a
cupboard.

'I am *not* sleeping in *that*,' I said firmly. 'No way.'

'Aw, come on honey,' Dad teased 'you'll love it. It'll be
fun.'

'I'd rather poke myself in the eye with a very sharp
stick,' I said, coldly.

We clacked across the tiled floor and went through a
door in the far corner. I watched the cupboard-thing warily
as I passed it, in case it attacked me.

The kitchen made Mom perk up some. It was OK, with
a microwave and a food processor and all the other useful
kitchen stuff she has back home, and had been extended in
back to make a real big family room.

Dad found the central heating boiler control and
switched it on, talking all the while. 'Don't worry, honey. If
there's *anything* you don't like, anything at all, we'll get it
fixed. I want you to be just as comfortable here as you
were back in the States.'

I noticed he wasn't saying 'back home' any more, and
that made me feel more out-of-place than ever.

Mom walked back into the main room, turning her coat collar up about her neck. 'Is any of this stuff antique, honey?' she asked. There was a familiar note in her voice.

'Certainly is,' Dad said, his voice echoing hollowly from the chimney where he was trying to light a fire that had been laid ready. 'There's not one thing here less than one hundred years old except the kitchen stuff and the central heating, and most of it's way older. This area is teeming with antique shops.'

Mom's eyes sparkled, and she ran her hand over the glossy, dark wood of the dining table. Inside my head, I groaned. I could feel one of Mom's Enthusiasms coming on.

Mom's Enthusiasms are a family joke. Mostly they don't last too long, but while they do, life can be real hard. The worst one, ever, was the musical saw. She heard some guy play one at a St Patrick's evening once, and she *had* to take lessons. *They* were OK—they were in the guy's home. But omigosh the practice! A musical saw played by a real whizz sounds kind of like someone screaming in tune. A musical saw played by my Mom sounded like someone being tortured.

Then there was the time we lived in an apartment and she wanted a garden, so she rented one from an old guy downtown who couldn't be bothered with his. She filled it with tomatoes and bell peppers and squash and stuff, and salad and flowers. She planted and dug and hoed and watered. Only as soon as things came good, the old guy she rented the garden from stole all the stuff and ate it. He said some kids had gotten in and smashed it all down, but Mum knew he'd had it. She said he still had tomato seeds stuck between his teeth! So Mom quit that, too. The Italian cookery Enthusiasm wasn't so bad, except eventually we

45

all got real sick of pasta, but she had to be talked out of keeping a Vietnamese pot-bellied pig. Now it looked like the next Enthusiasm was to be antiques . . .

'What's upstairs?' Jake mumbled. He mumbled because he'd opened up a tin box on the breakfast bar in the kitchen and found a huge fruitcake. He had a big mouthful and a great lump of it in his hand, too. Whoever'd laid the fire had left supplies for us, milk and other stuff so we wouldn't starve to death before we found the foodmarket.

'Come see!' Dad crowed.

He opened a door in the far wall of the kitchen, revealing a stone staircase laid with a carpet runner up the middle. Upstairs were four rooms, all the same size, and square, with a small hallway between, doors opening off it, and a bathroom built over the downstairs kitchen extension.

I went into the first room, next to the bathroom, the right-hand back bedroom, and stopped.

'Ooooh!' I said, completely forgetting that I wanted to go home to my pretty blue and white bedroom back in Pittsburgh. 'Oooh! I want this one! Pleeeease?'

The window was set low to the floor, in walls nearly a metre thick, with four square panes like a doll-house. It looked out across the clump of bent trees, small sandhills and dark rocks to the sea, a vast expanse of sparkling sapphire and jade flecked with white, a constantly moving picture. It took my breath away. It looked like it might be full of mermaids and sea-monsters, and a little way out in the bay the dark green, enticing hump of a small island crouched like a lion.

'Pleeeeease can I have this one? Please Dad?' I begged. My Dad grinned.

'Sure you can, sweetheart!'

Jake opened his mouth to object, then discovered that

the room next the bathroom on the other side opened on to the stairway on the outside of the house, and decided to settle for a private entrance instead. Mom and Dad's room had a view of rolling countryside, the distant rooftops of a small village, the bridge, and the river.

When I got tired of looking at the sea, I turned round and spotted the huge old fourposter bed, complete with drapes to pull cosily round. I guess my grin stretched from ear to ear.

I wrote a long letter to Kym that night. I told her the house was kind of spooky but not so bad, I had a genuine antique four post bed, with drapes, like in a movie; that we had our very own river, and that when I looked out of my bedroom window I could see the sea, and white seagulls riding on the wind.

I also said I missed her and all the guys back home, and I told her to spit in Kurt Bonadetti's eye for me if she saw him, the jerk.

CHAPTER THREE

The weather got warmer over the next couple of days, so I could go to the beach. I mostly had it to myself: Mom was off hunting antique shops, Jake was happy to sit up in the rocks with his Walkman and his GameBoy. I wandered along the shoreline, collecting shells (in a kid's pail: Mom got teed off at finding all my pockets full of sand), and watching the gulls wheel and soar like bits of blown paper in the wind. There were only a couple of weeks left to go of semester (I was going to have to learn to call it 'term') in the Pontpentre-dŵr Comprehensive School, so Dad said I could start in September, which was fine by me!

We didn't see too much of Dad—he was busy setting up Takahashi Electronics (Wales) Inc, and hiring folks. He left early in the morning before Jake and me were up, and came home mostly just in time to eat dinner with us. Sometimes we ate dinner in Aberaeron, and Jake and me soon learned that over here potato chips are called crisps and not the other way about, that jelly is jam, cookies are biscuits, stuff like that. Nobody speaks English too much round here. I began to get used to hearing Welsh spoken by people in shops and places, and even picked up a couple or three words. And I used them, too, which made people smile. They were kind of nice about it, and answered me slowly as if they actually wanted me to learn—so of course I tried harder, then.

Some days Mom drove us in the car, exploring. Once we got off our single track road onto the highway, we had to keep reminding Mom which side of the road she should be driving on: she was kind of absent minded about it, and me and Jake had to scream 'Left!!' at her a couple of times

48

before she got used to driving on the wrong side of the road. We wandered round some real old castles and towns, and I wrote Kym all about where I'd been, trying to make it sound real interesting so all the guys back home would be envious. But I hadn't heard a word yet from Kym, though I'd written twice already. Maybe she was real busy, or on vacation, something like that.

Mostly I went to the beach. The weather turned hot, and I was soon getting a tan despite the fifty-zillion protection factor sun cream Mom always insists I wear. It was on a hot, blue day, with barely any breeze from the sea, that I first met him.

I had my head down in a rock pool, investigating it. Now rock pools are real fascinating and the beach, Traeth Pontpentre-dŵr (it gets worse, don't it!) is full of them, and each one has tons of stuff in it, a dozen different kinds of green weed, tiny baby crabs, squishy dark red things that squirt water if you touch them, dark blue snaily things, pointed brown limpets, and once I even found a starfish.

I flipped a rock over, but there was nothing underneath, so I rinsed my sandy hands and stood up, stretching my aching back, ready to move on to the next pool.

'Put that rock back again after you turn it, girl. Otherwise everything on the underneath will die. Don't you even know that?'

His voice startled me so much that I lost my balance and sat down hard in the pool. Cold water was soaking through my shorts. I glared at him, but couldn't make out his face because the sun was shining in my eyes.

'Whyn't you just butt out?' I said angrily, scrambling to my feet. 'There was nothing under the darn rock to die.'

'Just because you can't *see* anything doesn't mean there's nothing there. The underside of each rock is

49

covered with microscopic life, and if you turn it up and expose it to the air, it will die.'

He moved round, out of the direct glare of the sun, and I saw a boy of about my own age, but a full foot taller, his brownish hair lightened by sun and sea into tousled, salty streaks. His eyes were pale, pale blue, almost colourless against his tan skin, and very unfriendly. Unsmiling, he watched me try to wring out my shorts and T-shirt. I tugged my baseball cap down over my eyes and glared at him.

'Boy, oh boy, you are such a buttinsky!' I snapped.

'Buttinsky? Oh, you mean I'm interfering. You might see it that way, but stupid, ignorant tourists like you can wreck the beach for us who live here.'

'Sheesh!' I stared at him. 'Are you always this rude, or are you making a special effort for me?'

'Why should I make any effort for you? *You* aren't important. You'll be gone in a week or so, I dare say, and a good job too. Tourists are a nuisance.'

I scowled. 'That's all you know, smartypants. I'm no tourist. I live here. My Mom and Dad and my brother and me all live in the Toll House, so . . .' I stuck my tongue out, then wished I hadn't.

'Oh, one of the Yanks from the Toll House, are you? Coming here, throwing your weight about . . .? Can't live without central heating and hot showers. Soft, the lot of you.' Then he just turned right round and strode off across the sand, leaving me soggy, sandy, and boiling with fury. Interfering know-it-all!

Nevertheless, as soon as he was out of sight, I turned the rock back over the way it was, just in case there *were* millions of tiny microscopic animals and stuff gasping their last breath on account of me.

Dad laughed when I told him about the boy that night

over dinner in the hotel in Aberaeron. Mrs Pugh, the owner's wife, was serving our dessert at the time, and overheard. She smiled.

'That'll be young Twm ap Hywel, I expect. Always has been a bit outspoken, our Twm. Considers the sea and the shoreline his own responsibility, he does. He's like an unpaid warden. Picks up all the litter the trippers leave behind, and keeps an eye on the shore for hurt birds and animals. A very serious boy, that one. His Taid says he's been here before, knows too much for it to be his first time round on this earth!'

'Tide?' I said, puzzled. 'What's a Tide?'

'Taid,' Mrs Pugh corrected me. 'Grandfather. Lovely old man, gentle soul. Brought Twm and his little brother up since his Mam left.'

'I'm not surprised his Mom left,' I retorted, 'if he tried to boss her the way he did me! Who does he think he is, chewing me out that way!'

Mrs Pugh gave me an extra dollop of cream on my apple pie. 'He's probably the next best thing to Royalty round here, is young Twm,' she said seriously. 'People listen to him. And his Taid.'

'Royalty?' I was puzzled. 'Oh, Mrs Pugh, you're putting me on!'

'Indeed I am not, Catrin. Twm's Grandfather, Taid Hywel, says he can trace his ancestry back to Owain Glyndŵr—and beyond, it's said, to Merlin himself. Twm's in direct descent. Not only Glyndŵr, who was nearly royalty, but to one of the Old Ones into the bargain—who definitely *were* Royalty round by here!'

She put the cream jug on the table, and Jake reached for it greedily. Mom rapped his knuckles with her spoon. 'You have enough cream, Jake. Don't be greedy.'

Jake pulled a face, and laughing, Mrs Pugh headed for the kitchen. 'Ought to listen to Twm, Catrin,' she said over her shoulder. 'He's a lovely boy, and worth listening to. You'll learn ever such a lot. What he doesn't know about the sea isn't worth knowing, and that's a fact.'

'I sincerely doubt that!' I muttered under my breath so that she wouldn't hear. Did she really expect me to believe that total no-hope buttinsky, that swollen-headed interfering *creep* was a magician or something? For Pete's sake! Come on! What am I, emerald green or something?

I filled my mouth with sweet apple pie and cream, and spoke indistinctly through it. 'Sheesh, Dad, does she think I'm dumb? Merlin the Magician? Aw, he's just something Disney dreamed up for—what was it?—*The Sword in the Stone*.'

Dad shook his head, laughing. 'Not in Wales, honey. Some say this is where Merlin came from, around here. Why, one of the guys I hired for Takahashi was telling me just last week that in Carmarthen there used to be the remains of an old tree the locals called "Merlin's Oak". Legend had it that if the oak was felled, Carmarthen town would fall, too. It used to stand slap in the middle of the main street, large as life, with all the traffic driving round it.'

I looked disbelievingly at him. 'And when they chopped it down? What? Earthquakes? Typhoons? Come on, Dad. You're putting me on!'

Dad shook his head, seriously. 'They kept that old hunk of tree wrapped in iron bands until it was nothing but splinters, until they finally moved it to make way for a new road. They didn't chop it down, though, honey. They very carefully moved it to the local Museum. They take Merlin real serious around here.'

'Huh.' I finished my pie in silence. They were all

52

putting me on, and Dad was as bad as the rest of them. Merlin. Magic. Hah!

I wrote to Kym again that night. That made three letters I'd mailed her so far, and I still hadn't had one in return. She must have gone away on vacation—although her folks usually didn't. Well, I guess she'd write soon. I was still homesick for Pittsburgh—but the sun and the sand and the sea were working their magic on me, and I was beginning to fall in love with Wales just a little bit, so I only moped for Pittsburgh when the weather was wet and I couldn't find anything to watch on the lousy four-channel TV.

Jake made friends with a kid from the village—Cei, who had a tooth missing in front, and fair, almost white hair that stuck out. Cei had a passion for fishing, and they disappeared for hours, returning when they were hungry, soaking wet, occasionally with a small brown trout, usually with nothing. Mom invited Cei to tea one day, and he turned up neatly dressed, his white-blonde hair slicked flat, looking not one bit like everyday untidy Cei.

'My brother will fetch me, after,' he said. My Mom made a traditional American feast with fudge brownies and chocolate chip cookies and potato chips and hot dogs, and Cei ate and ate and ate until his face was all round and shiny with food, like a hamster. When tea was over, the boys went up to Jake's room, after which there was mostly just the sound of electronic machines bleeping, and lots of giggles and thumps.

Eight o'clock on the dot, there was a knock at the door. My Mom's Enthusiasm had uncovered a dragon's head door-knocker, and its shattering crash about gave us all a heart-attack, even though it had been up a week and the mail-lady rat-tatted on it every morning. Never bringing a letter from Kym, though.

I left my book and unlatched the heavy door. Outside, looking real awkward, was the boy from the beach. He was blushing, although he looked me straight in the eye.

'I've come for my brother. Please,' he added as an afterthought.

'Cei is your brother? But he seemed so *nice!*' I said, sarcastically.

Dad's hand closed firmly on my shoulder, reminding me that good manners to guests is the house rule, whoever the visitor is, even if you *hate* him (which I did). 'Come in, lad. Cei's upstairs.'

Twm's voice was so quiet that he was almost whispering. 'Thank you, Sir, but I will not come in.'

My Dad looked surprised. 'Why not? Hey, it's real draughty in here with the door open. Aw, come on in. Have a coke and a cookie while you're waiting for Cei.' And Dad stood back, frowning slightly. I smirked inside myself. Good. Now Dad knew how rude Twm could be. He could just stay outside and freeze if that was what he wanted.

Still Twm hesitated, and still my father beckoned him inside. Mom joined us at the front door. 'Won't you come in, Twm? Please, at least sit a spell. Cei won't be long. They're in the middle of a game, and it's not fair to hustle them. Please?'

I couldn't believe they were begging him like that! Three times they asked him. At last, reluctantly, with a real weird expression on his face, (like he was stepping into a black hole or something) Twm stepped over the threshhold. His pale, dark-lashed eyes met mine.

And everything changed. I blinked, looked at him, and my mouth sagged open. In the split second it took for his shadow to cross the slab of grey-black slate that formed the doorstep of the Toll House, he changed from a real nasty boy to something quite different. His brown, sun-streaked hair took on a sheen of reddish gold. Already taller than me, he seemed taller still, and for a brief instant—I must have been dreaming. Maybe I'd gotten too much sun—he seemed to be dressed in old-fashioned clothes, as if he had stepped out of a fairy tale. His eyes were still on me, with a curious, half-worried, half-excited expression.

I tried to move backward, away from him, but tripped over one of the wretched little rugs and landed once more on my butt. It seemed every time I met him I did a pratfall. I didn't get up, I just sat there, staring up at him, and almost unwillingly, he held out his hand to help me up.

I put out my own hand. Our fingers touched, and—almost like treading on a stair that isn't there, or having one of those half-asleep dreams when your whole body jerks and you wake up—everything kind of jolted back to normal again. I saw him as he had been before: untidy, a bit sullen, ordinary. I closed my mouth. I must have been dreaming.

'Thanks,' I said, crossly, and allowed him to haul me up.

Cei and Jake came tumbling down the stairs making rifle-shooting noises, both collapsing in a heap at the foot, pretending to be dead cowboys or Indians or something.

'Cei!' Twm said sharply, and Cei immediately leapt to his feet, grinning and shoving his hair back from his eyes.

'I'm ready, Twm,' he said. 'I got all my stuff together.'

'Twm?' Dad said. 'Twm ap Hywel?'

Twm nodded. 'Yes sir.'

'Well, well!' Dad said, rubbing his hands together 'We were just talking about you the other evening with Mrs Pugh at the Market Arms.'

Twm smiled. It was a polite smile, and didn't reach his eyes. 'Saying nice things, sir, I hope.' But I got the

55

impression he really didn't care what Mrs Pugh had said about him. Like it wasn't important what anybody else thought.

Dad grinned and tapped him lightly on the shoulder with his balled fist. 'All very good stuff, Twm.'

When they were ready to leave, I found my eyes meeting Twm's again. His were confused, questioning, and forgetting that I really did not like him *one little bit*, I followed him to the gate. He ushered Cei ahead of him through it, then turned round.

'I don't know how to tell you this,' he said urgently. 'Or even if I *should* tell you, but you are the One. Your name is Catrin, isn't it?'

I nodded. I guess my mouth was open again. 'One?' I said, stupidly. 'What One? Who?'

'The One with the Signs!' he whispered, his eyes glowing. 'I don't know what will happen. But something will. Trust me. You *are* the One.'

'You're nuts.' I said, shaking my head sadly. 'Totally dingdongdoodle.'

He made an odd little noise in his throat, half way between exasperation and anger. 'I expect I do sound mad,' he said. 'But you'll see, soon. In the meantime, take care who you invite inside your home. Not everyone round here is friendly, and if you are the One, then you must be careful.'

'I'm sure they aren't all friendly,' I said. 'Some of them are even nuts!'

'Listen, Catrin. Three times your parents invited me: twice I refused, for fear of danger. The third time, the Old Law made me accept. Whoever comes to your house, ask them in once only, ever. If they refuse, take their refusal and accept it. Do not *ever* ask three times. You don't know who you are asking.'

'*Old Law?*' I said. This guy was, like, away with the fairies! He turned away.

'If you need help, find me,' he said. 'I am usually on the *traeth*. I will do what I can to guide you—but if you are the One, the Signs are yours.' And taking Cei's hand, he strode off down the sandy towpath towards the village.

I shut my gaping mouth for the third time in a half-hour and slowly went inside. Royalty or magicians Twm might have in his ancestry—but I was pretty sure he had a fruitcake or two, also!

CHAPTER FOUR

Yup, a total fruitcake. All those m-m-mysterious warnings! Who was he trying to kid? I wrote Kym all about him, made it sound real jokey. I finished up, 'and don't forget you promised you'd write. I've written four letters and you didn't send one in return yet. Hope your hands didn't drop off!!!!!' Then, just so she'd know I wasn't being mean, I finished up 'Just joking!!! Write soooooon!!!'

Then I took it downstairs and put it on the hall stand Mom had found in a 'Shoppe'. She looked up from *The Antique Hunter's Guide*. She was so caught up in her Enthusiasm she kept reading chunks of it aloud to us. We'd all learned to look like we were listening, and say 'Wow!' and 'You don't say,' in all the right places.

'Did Kym write back yet, honey?' she asked. I shook my head.

'That's sad. I have a feeling you're a better friend to Kym than she ever has been to you. And she was always so unkind to her Mom and Dad—that's not nice.'

I felt my face get red. Inside me, I agreed with Mom— but I had to stick up for Kym.

'Hey, Mom. That's not true. Kym's a real kind person. It's just her Mom and Dad embarrass her.'

'Everyone's Mom and Dad embarrass them sometime, honey. They just don't go telling all their friends about it the whole time. Family is family, and even if you don't always agree, you stick up for each other with outsiders.'

'I'm not an outsider, Mom. I'm her best friend.'

'Your Dad and Jake and me are outsiders, and she's always saying how fat her Mom is, or how boring her Dad is. You and Jake wouldn't do that, would you? No way!'

I wanted to stick up for Kym, but I was beginning to wonder if she really was my friend. Maybe she was just a 'fairweather friend' who couldn't be bothered to write me.

Sunday night, Dad and Mom decided we should all go to Church. Back home, we were Episcopalian, and I went quite often, because I liked it, but Jake didn't. He pulled a face, but Dad was firm.

'The church is part of Welsh life—or it used to be. I think it would be kind of nice to go while we're here—touch base with the locals.'

'We touch base in the Market Arms, don't we, Dad?' Jake said mischievously, and Dad grinned.

'Sure we do. But these are the *Sunday* folks!'

The tiny church was real old, built of rough stone, and there were brass plates in the walls remembering people, and gravestones on the floor of the aisle. I tried not to walk on them, because it felt kind of wrong to walk around on dead people, but if I took a giant step to avoid one, I usually landed on another. There was a wonderful wooden ceiling, rounded, like the inside of a barrel, and it smelled of furniture polish and flowers. The service was all in Welsh, but the Minister found us a prayer book that had Welsh on the left side of the page, and English on the right, so I could translate as I went along.

We all kind of struggled with the hymns, though. It was real frustrating—we knew most all the tunes from back home, but we couldn't make the Welsh words fit! I decided I was gonna have to find out how to pronounce written-down Welsh, even if I couldn't understand it.

After, people crowded round in a real friendly manner to say hello, and I realised Dad was right. Somehow, by coming to the service, we'd shown the local people that we were serious about sharing their community. I hung about on the edge of the little clump of folks around Mom and Dad, then something made me turn.

Twm stood by the church door, staring at me. He jerked his head for me to follow, and I slipped away and joined him outside the door.

'I've only got a minute,' he said, urgently. 'You've got to listen to me, Catrin.'

Naturally, my back went up. 'I don't *got to* do anything!' I retorted, and turned to go.

He caught my arm, pulling me back. 'Please, Catrin.' he said, and unwillingly, I stopped. 'Listen to me. It's important. Please?'

'I'm listening,' I said, kind of sullenly.

'I told you things will be happening. If you are the One, you will find the first Sign very soon.'

'What sign? What am I supposed to look for?'

He pushed his fingers through his hair, making it stand on end, his brown face anxious. 'I don't know. But there will be a Sign, if you are the One. And if you find it, be careful. They will try to take it back.'

I stared at him. 'Are you nuts? What am I supposed to be looking for, doing, anything? Who is "they"? I'm not important.'

'The wild things tell me. The birds and the animals. *They* know. Please, Catrin? Trust me.'

By now I was absolutely certain he was, like, totally insane, but I nodded. 'I trust you. I'll look for the sign— whatever it is. But what is it?'

He stared at me, as if he was searching for something in my face.

'For anything, Catrin. Anything that is different, or strange, that calls to you. D'you understand?'

'Nope,' I said. 'But I'll look—and listen in case anything calls.'

My parents were coming.

'I've got to go,' he said. 'I'll see you soon.' And he was gone, slipping into the night like a ghost.

'Was that Twm?' Mom said. 'He's a strange boy, that one. But I think I like him.'

I thought I did, too. Except he was nuts!

I lay wide awake that night, listening to the surf crashing on the shore fifty metres away, and wondering. Back home in Pittsburgh, mysteries and magic are safely shut up in storybooks, like ghosts and ghouls on Hallowe'en. But Wales was kind of different, somehow. It's so old it makes magic and stuff seem believable. Like the church—it's older than *America*! All those people, all those centuries, getting born, getting christened, getting married, getting buried, saying their prayers, and all the time America hadn't even been *discovered* yet.

I woke up to rain. Not a satisfying downpour, just a thin, ratty, miserable drizzle.

'Right,' Mom said briskly after breakfast 'When I've loaded the dishwasher, you guys are going shopping.'

'Shopping?' Jake said, suspiciously, for next to the dentist, Jake hates shopping. 'What for, Mom?'

'Well,' Mom said. 'When Catrin starts her new school, she'll need hockey kit and a schoolbag, and—um—a uniform.'

'A what?' I said, slowly. 'I do not believe I am hearing this, Mom. I am *not* gonna wear any dumb UNIFORM! You have to find me another school!' Back home we all wore what we wanted to school—usually jeans and T-shirts. Only the real no-hope girly girls that giggled if a guy so much as looked at them wore skirts. But a uniform? No way!

Jake held his stomach and mouthed a 'Ho-ho-ho' at me, like a skinny Santa Claus.

'—and Jake needs black school shoes. They don't allow sneakers over here.' That wiped the grin off Jake's face. He'd wear his sneakers in bed if Mom would allow him. 'And there aren't any other schools—unless you want to be a boarder.'

I did not.

We went into Cardigan for the uniform and the shoes. Mom said we'd buy Jake's shoes first, then my uniform (I was still trying to think of ways of getting out of uniform—burn the store down? Or maybe the school?), then we'd all go eat lunch in a burger place. We went to every shoe store in town, where Jake said every pair of black, laced-up shoes he tried was way too big, or way too small, or rubbed in the heel. Eventually Mom lost her cool.

'Come hell or high holidays, Jacob Rhys Morgan, you are gonna have black school shoes by the time we leave this store! Wear sneakers to school and you get suspended. So make up your mind right now that you *will* have black school shoes. And until you choose a pair, and I pay for them, and I walk out of this store with a pair of black shoes under my arm, NOBODY GETS TO EAT!'

That did it. Jake meekly picked up the first pair of shoes the assistant had brought. 'I guess these fit OK,' he mumbled. Mom paid, Jake hung his head and sulked, and as we left the store, Mom winked at me over his head.

'OK,' Mom said. 'Now for you, Cat. The store where we get your stuff is right across the way.'

The uniform wasn't too, totally, gross. At least it didn't have one of those tunic things or a tie. When I'd put on the straight dark green skirt and the white open-necked shirt under a red and dark-green sweatshirt, I thought I looked real neat. Anyway, if everyone else had to wear the same kind of clothes, well, nobody would look any grosser than anyone else, would they?'

The storelady put her head on one side. 'Colour's lovely on you, with that hair,' she said. 'Colours of the Welsh flag, red, green and white.' While she was packing up what we'd bought, Mom checked her shopping list and saw we still had to buy black panty-hose (they call them tights over here). We bought those quickly, and then headed for a burger place downtown. When we'd finished eating, the annoying drizzlesome rain had stopped, so we went for a walk around Cardigan before heading for home. Jake wanted to go see the market, so we went in, and Mom turned him loose to go look at the mice and stuff like that, and Mom and me went downstairs to where the bookstalls and antiques were.

Up in one corner of the basement we found not so much a store, or even a stall, just a single, poky little room. Mom spotted the 'darling little escritoire' right off. The bent, white-bearded old guy in charge called it a 'writing desk, Madam'.

Mom set about crawling on the floor underneath it looking at joints and corners and talking rapid fire about dovetails, and tenons and mortices, and mitres, referring to her pocket antiques book (the big one wouldn't fit in anything but a suitcase), and totally bewildering the old guy, who looked about a hundred-and-ninety, and could hardly bend, let alone get down on the floor to see what she was getting so excited about.

I soon got bored and left her to it, wandering to the back of the little shop to have a poke around on my own account. It was kind of dark back there, and a bit dusty. Racks of musty old clothes, old christening gowns, nightdresses and underskirts in yellowing white cotton, piles of cracked china, huge old gramophone discs, wind-up gramophones with huge horns to go with them, piles of sheet music, chamber pots, hat boxes, jewellery and feather boas. Amongst them jostled a small rectangular box about half the size of a shoebox.

OK—I'm a longnose, I admit it. I come from a long line of longnoses. I picked it up and lifted the lid. Inside, wrapped in silky fabric, was something smooth and egg-shaped. Carefully I lifted it out and unwrapped it, holding it towards the light so that I could see it better.

When the last layer of silky stuff slid away, in my hand was the most beautiful thing I'd ever seen. It was oval and about twice the size of a chicken egg. It didn't look like it had been painted—an old woman in the next apartment to us back home used to collect stones and paint them with flowers and stuff. This wasn't a bit like those. It was the most exquisite, iridescent blue I've ever seen, like a butterfly wing or a bubble, and yet not like either. The colour was more like the rainbow colours that oil makes in a puddle when the sun catches it, only a million times better: gleaming, shining, mostly blue but a whole stack of other colours too, shifting and changing as light caught it. I curved my hand round it: it was warm.

I suddenly understood my Mom's Enthusiasms. I REALLY HAD TO HAVE THIS STONE! I had about five hundred dollars in Granny's Splurge Account (Granny pays money into the account once a year, just for me to splurge on anything at all I want). Trouble was, I didn't think even the Queen of England had enough money to buy this. It had to be priceless. It was like a giant, multi-coloured jewel. So what was it doing in a shabby little market back room?

'Mom?' I said, and she squirmed backwards out from under the writing desk, dusting off her knees.

'What do you have, honey?' she asked.

I showed her the stone. 'I'd really, really like to have this, Mom, if I have enough in my splurge account. Please?' That's the only condition Granny put on the Account, that I check with Mom before I buy anything.

Mom shrugged. 'It's only an old painted pebble, honey, hardly worth anything. You really want that?' I stared at her. Old painted pebble? I held it up to the light so the colours shimmered and danced. 'Mom! Old pebble? Are you nuts? Just look at it!'

The old man took an interest. 'You see what you see, *cariad*,' he said softly. 'Some see an old painted paperweight. Some see different.' He looked hard at me, his blue eyes vivid against his white hair and beard. 'If the young lady sees something she likes, who are we to argue? Were you wanting the desk, then, Madam?'

My Mom's eyes narrowed. This was the bit she liked best, the bargaining. 'How much?' she asked slowly.

The old guy narrowed his eyes too, as if he was trying to work out how much my Mom could afford to pay. They looked like a pair of gunfighters getting ready to draw and shoot it out.

'Three hundred,' he said, 'and I'll include the paperweight for the little girl.'

Normally I would have called him on that. Little girl! But I wanted the marvellous stone, so I couldn't upset him, could I?

'Two-fifty,' Mom haggled. 'And not a cent more. Including the paperweight!'

They were nose to nose now, staring each other down.

The old man smiled, and his eyes twinkled. 'Plenty of money, you Americans. Beautiful piece of furniture, that writing desk. Georgian. Could even be earlier.'

'Victorian,' my Mom snapped. 'Two-fifty. My last offer.'

'You'll likely ruin me, Madam,' he said, but his heart didn't seem to be in it.

Mom didn't say anything.

'Two-seventy-five?' said the old guy.

'Two-fifty,' Mom replied, frowning, 'including the pebble.'

'All right,' the old guy sighed, and Mom wrote the cheque. Strangely, he ignored Mom after that. He re-wrapped the beautiful egg, put it in the box and placed the box in my hands.

'Use it well,' he said, softly.

Use it? I stared at him. Then I realised he thought it was a paperweight.

'Oh, yeah, sure I will,' I said. 'You bet.'

The old man took the cheque from Mom's hand, but his eyes were still on me. Against the light coming from outside in the main market hall, his white hair looked like a dandelion puff.

'You have the Look!' he whispered.

Was *everybody* nuts around here?

CHAPTER FIVE

'Dad's home already!' I said, spotting his car in the drive when we got home. 'He's never home this early.'

'He is today,' Mom said, opening the front door.

Dad came out of the kitchen, closing the door behind him. He had a peculiar expression, kinda 'I got a secret'-ish. I looked at Mom just in time to see her raise her eyebrows, and Dad nod back.

'What's going on, you guys?' I asked. Dad opened the kitchen door. Jake, puzzled, went past him into the kitchen, and I put the box with the stone in it on the old black dresser and followed. Jake squeaked.

In a wicker basket beside the big red Aga stove was a black and white puppy, sound asleep. Jake's wanted a dog since forever, but it wouldn't have been fair to keep one in the city. We both got down on our knees beside the basket.

'Thanks, Dad!' Jake said, his eyes shining. 'Oh, gee, Mom, thanks. I'm sorry I was such a jerk about my school shoes.'

'He's a Welsh border collie,' Dad said. 'A sheep-dog. Very intelligent. He'll have to be exercised and trained, though. He's not a toy to be picked up and forgotten.'

I lifted a soft, floppy ear and tickled it, and the puppy yawned, revealing sharp needle teeth and a curved pink tongue. It opened its eyes and blinked. So did I, because I'd expected brown eyes—but they were almost the same colour as Twm's, with a dark line around the iris.

'Look at his eyes, Dad!' I gasped.

'I know, weird eyes, right?' Dad said. 'I guess that's one reason why you've got him. The mother had four pups, three bitches and one dog. The bitches all have ordinary brown eyes. The farmer said he preferred to train bitches, they are more obedient—but I think he just didn't want a fey dog.'

The puppy clambered out of the basket, stretched, flopped down on his fat rear end, gazing at Jake and me intently, his ridiculous little tail wagging furiously. As if he had come to a decision, he waddled towards me, and climbed onto my knees, looking up into my face. I bent my head and he licked my nose.

'What's "fey", Dad?' Jake asked.

'Kind of magical, son. "Fey". A bit spooky, I guess.'

I wasn't quite sure what Dad meant—but he was sure magical to me!

Jake stroked the pup. 'What we gonna call him, Catty?' he asked.

'Has to be something Welsh,' Mom said, and we all agreed.

We racked our brains. 'Sion?' Dad said.

'Dafydd,' Mom suggested

'Ffred!' Jake said.

'Tudor? Like the Welsh princes?'

'No, Llewelyn. Or Gwynfor. Or Maldwyn, or Pugh—'

'Pooh?'

'Pugh!'

We argued right through dinner, and after, we went walking on the beach before it got dark, the whole family and our dog. It was real nice to have Dad home in time to tag along.

The puppy romped down the path ahead of us and through the dunes, sniffing and investigating everything that grew, shifted in the wind, or just lay there minding its own business. Until he came face to face with the sea.

He stood dead still and stared at it, then slowly trotted to meet the incoming tide. He tasted the white foam, sneezed, then waded out a few steps, gazing out to sea, for all the world like a sailor on lookout.

'That's it!' Dad said. 'What about calling him Madoc?'

'My Dog?' Jake said, puzzled. 'That's some weird name for a dog, Dad. Of course he's our dog!'

'Not "My Dog", Jake. Madoc!' Dad repeated. 'Madoc was a medieval Welsh Prince. Some folks believe he discovered America—in 1170, three hundred years before Christopher Columbus! The way that pup is acting, he's a sea-dog all right!'

'Madoc?' I called. The puppy turned, grinning. 'He likes it!' I said. 'Hey, Madoc!'

Much later that night, I remembered my stone, and got it from the dresser to show Jake and Dad.

'Catrin fell in love with it,' Mom said. 'She found it in a little antiques place in Cardigan.'

Jake said 'Mega-boring, Cat! You're real weird,' so I stuck my tongue out at him.

Dad turned the stone over, feeling the smoothness of it, but it was obvious that *he* couldn't see the beautiful colours either. 'I can see why you wanted it, honey,' he said at last, but I could tell he was only being tactful. 'It's been painted up real nice, and it has a good cool feel to it. Yeah. It's good.'

He tossed it to me, and I caught it in mid air, light tumbling off the colours. Dad was wrong, though. It wasn't cool. It was warm, as if it had been lying in the sun all day, or in the warm nest of some beautiful bird. I took it up to bed with me, putting it on the broad windowsill where the sun would catch it. How come only I could see how beautiful it was? What was wrong with Mom and Dad's eyesight?

69

Next day, the rain had cleared, so me and Jake took Madoc to the beach to start training him. Madoc watched us with his pale, intelligent eyes, listened to our commands—and did the exact opposite!

Eventually, with Jake pushing his butt end down, he kinda got the general idea. Then, suddenly, he curled up and went to sleep.

'I guess dogs get bored, too,' Jake said, and wandered off to sit on the rocks with his Walkman. I sat beside Madoc and read my book, enjoying the sun, the sea and the small creature curled at my feet. I couldn't ever remember feeling quite so happy in my whole life. Yet only a couple of weeks ago I'd been in a real snit about coming here! Kind of hard to believe, now. Twm and his warnings had flown right out of my head.

When Madoc yawned and stretched, I put my book in my pocket and we headed for home. Mom was baking. She'd been real busy, and there were not only brownies but cheese buns, angelfood cake and Welsh cakes. She'd wheedled the recipe from Mrs Pugh at the Market Arms by trading it for hers for blueberry muffins.

I stole one of the flat, golden-brown cakes, still warm from the griddle, and sat on the rag rug to share it with Madoc. The phone rang, and Mom's hands were floury, so I got it.

'Hi, Dad,' I said. 'What's new?'

'Lots of things,' he answered solemnly. 'New moons, new pennies, new shoes, New Years and New Clear Physics.' Which probably sounds totally insane, but it's a family thing, OK?

'Can I talk to Mom, honey?' he went on.

'She's kind of tied up, Dad. She has her hands in cookie dough. Is it important?'

''Fraid so. Ask her if she can wash her hands and come talk to me.'

I called, 'He needs to talk to you, Mom.'

She rinsed her hands and I wondered what was so important it couldn't be relayed through me. I listened in to Mom's end of the conversation, but ended up even more mystified.

'Hi, honey. Who? What? Oh! When!'

I could hear Dad's voice rumbling in the background. Then

'Whaaat? Saturday? Omigosh, David! You can't do this to me!'

Dad said something else, and Mom gave in. 'Well, all right. But you have to be here too. I don't even know her!'

'Know who?' I asked when she hung up.

'A visitor,' Mom said, pulling a face. 'Kinda the local lady of the manor—she owned the land the new factory's built on. Dad met her today, and he's only invited her to tea, Saturday!'

When Dad got home that night, we wanted to know everything. 'Is she real rich, Dad?' Jake asked hopefully.

'After selling a chunk of land to Mr Takahashi, I don't think she has to worry about where her next meal comes from, Jake,' Dad laughed. 'She's a kind of formidable old lady: she had her driver bring her to the factory gates— nobody knew she was coming. Then she demanded to be let in to see me. She'd done her homework—asked for me by name, according to the security guard. He says she "keeps herself to herself", so nobody knows her too well. I guess it's something of an honour to have her come to tea with us.'

Mom sighed. 'Sure it is, honey. But if she's so grand, what on earth possessed you to invite her here? Couldn't we have taken her someplace instead?'

'She more or less invited herself,' Dad said. 'All I said was, "you must meet my family some time", like you do, being polite, y'know? And the next thing she said was "I shall come to tea on Saturday. You may expect me at four." Anyway,' he went on 'I'm proud of my family—she should consider herself real lucky to meet you.'

'Aah—I'm going out, Saturday,' Jake said, quickly. 'I promised Cei I'd go fish.'

'Uh-huh!' Mom said, sweetly, shaking her head. 'Saturday afternoon, you stay home. And you don't get to wear levis, and you behave real good, Jake my boy.' Mom leaned forward until her nose was about a half-inch from Jake's. 'Or you shall be grounded until you take root and grow little apples!'

'Aw, Mom!' Jake muttered.

I didn't want to go out—I wanted to see a real lady of the manor! Mom pasted on a cheesy fake smile and said 'I guess it'll be kind of nice to have a sweet little old lady come visit. Give us a chance to put on our best bibs and tuckers. Cucumber sandwiches and cups of Earl Grey tea!'

Cucumber sandwiches—hah! You'd have thought maybe the Queen of England was coming to tea! Mom cleaned, polished, swept, dusted, pored over cookbooks, rearranged the furniture, put it back again the way it was before, changed the curtains, took Jake to get his hair cut, and bought me a new dress to wear, because last time I'd worn my 'good dress' I'd been about six inches shorter and a whole lot narrower. All day Friday and Saturday morning she about wore us all to sticks fussing at us, and yelling instructions at us from the kitchen while she cooked stuff.

Saturday was Mrs Gwynne-Davies's chauffeur's day off, so Dad had to collect her. Now when my Dad gets annoyed, or has to try real hard to keep his temper about something, he pushes his fingers through his hair in front so that it stands up, like a cockatoo's crest.

I was peeking through the front window when Dad got back. His hair was standing right on end. Mom, Jake and I rushed to the front door, and saw Dad open the back door of the car for our visitor. Maybe he was mad because she'd ridden in back, and made him feel like the hired help. I followed Mom and Jake out to greet our visitor.

All I could see at first was the top of a snowy white head with pink scalp showing through. She sat in the car doorway, and Dad reached in to help her out.

'I can manage, young man,' she said. 'Do you think I'm helpless?' and she whacked his ankle with her walking cane.

Mom whispered 'Oh-oooh! I think we're gonna have a real fun time, kids,' and Jake groaned.

When the old lady straightened up, well! I know it's not kind, and homely folks sometimes have real nice natures to make up, but! She was the UGLIEST little old lady I ever did see! She had a big nose, and a square jaw, and dark eyebrows that met in the middle and didn't match her frizzly white hair. Her eyes were like mean little black beads. And there was a wart on her chin. With hairs.

'Omigosh!' Jake muttered. 'It's a witch!'

'No!' I whispered back. 'She's not a witch. She's a troll! There's gonna be a troll in the Troll House, Jake!' We grinned at each other.

Mom dug me in the ribs, hissing 'Behave, you kids!' but I could see she was laughing inside. She stuck out her arm to help Mrs Gwynne-Davies up the path, but got the cane waved at her.

'Welcome!' Mom said, weakly, 'Won't you come inside?'

'That's what I'm here for, isn't it?' said our visitor.

'Best behaviour, Mom!' Jake whispered, and Mom aimed a pretend swipe at his head behind the old lady's back.

CHAPTER SIX

She was awful! She chose to sit next the fire. Mom offered her coffee.

'Tea,' the old lady snapped. 'Two spoons of sugar, and be sure the milk goes in first.'

As Mom went into the kitchen she pulled a long face. I followed her out.

'Mom, she's awful!' I whispered, and Mom nodded.

'Mary Poppins she ain't,' she said.

'Dear Little Old Lady she ain't!' I whispered, and Mom had to cover her mouth to keep from laughing out loud.

Mom made proper tea, with a pot, instead of making it in mugs, and put cookies on a pretty plate on a tray. She forgot the milk-in-first bit when she poured the tea, began to pour it away, but then shrugged, added the milk and gave the tea a quick stir to mix it. 'She'll never know the difference!' We grinned at each other wickedly.

Mom gave Mrs Gwynne-Davies her cup, and I watched as she raised it to her lips, her pinkie finger crooked. She slurped. Jake's eyes bulged like a bullfrog's.

'Milk in first, milk in first!' the old woman said, angrily. 'You put the milk in afterwards.'

Mom turned red. Trouble was, she couldn't deny it!

The old lady glared at Jake. 'Don't stare, boy. It's rude.' Jake turned scarlet, and studied his feet. 'How old is the girl?' She nodded at me, as if I were a bunch of bananas.

'Catrin's fourteen, rising fifteen, and Jake is nine,' Dad said, proudly.

'Very thin, isn't she? Pity about that hair.' Mrs Gwynne-Davies curled her lip. 'Not attractive, ginger hair. Still, she can dye it when she is old enough.'

Now my Mom is *real* hot on personal comments, and I was waiting for her to blow, but she didn't. She just went kind of red and didn't say anything. I opened and shut my mouth like a goldfish, wishing I could say what I was thinking. For the record, I do not have ginger hair. My hair is auburn. *Dark* auburn. I scowled.

Mom sat down as if her knees had given way, and I sat uncomfortably beside Dad and Jake on the high-backed wooden settle, like three chimpanzees in a row.

'I don't trust Americans,' the old lady went on. 'I don't know why I agreed to sell the land for that wretched factory. Americans are unreliable. Always late for everything. Look at the War!'

Excuse me? The war? Mom's face was now dark red, and if she'd been that mad at me, I'd have taken cover in the nearest hurricane shelter. Dad was watching Mom kind of helplessly, as if he was waiting for her to explode, too. She took a deep breath, and opened her mouth.

'Won't you try a cucumber sandwich, Mrs Gwynne-Davies,' she said sweetly. 'Or perhaps a chocolate brownie. They're very good!'

Way to go, Mom, I thought. Show the old bat *you* have manners if she doesn't!

Mrs Gwynne-Davies was little, old and frail, with an appetite just like a bird's. Yeah, sure! A vulture! She gobbled up everything in sight. Afterwards, she levered herself to her feet, spilling brownie crumbs all over, and leaned on her stick.

'Where is the W.C.?' she demanded.

'The who?' Mom asked.

'The lavatory!' the woman snapped. 'The toilet, the— what is it you mealy-mouthed Americans call it? Oh, yes. The powder room.'

'Upstairs, I'm afraid,' Mom said. 'I hope you can manage the stairs.'

'Of course I can manage stairs,' she said. 'Do you think I'm helpless?'

I showed her the bathroom. Once she was inside, I slipped into my room and sat on my bed waiting for the toilet to flush so that I could help her downstairs, although I felt more like pushing her! I was still smarting from that 'ginger hair' remark!

I didn't hear the bathroom door open. First I knew, she was standing in my bedroom! She looked kind of startled to see me.

'Are you ready to go downstairs?' I asked, coldly. How dare she snoop in *my* room?

'N-no,' she stammered. 'Er—there isn't a towel.'

'Sure there is,' I said. I knew Mom had put out a fluffy blue one. I peeked into the bathroom. The rail was empty.

'Gee, I'm sorry,' I said, mystified. 'I was sure Mom'd . . . I'll go fetch one.' When I got back, the old lady was standing in the door of the bathroom. She snatched the towel from my hands, went in and locked the door behind her. I wandered back into my bedroom until I heard the door open again. Then I noticed that my beautiful stone egg had disappeared! Only Mrs Gwynne-Davies could have taken it. But why? And how could I get it back? She was a guest, for Petesake. Mom and Dad would never forgive me if I called her on it, and would probably ground me for life. I stared at her, suspiciously. She clutched her large brown purse—handbags, they call them here. She looked kind of smug and satisfied.

'Downstairs!' she said, imperiously, and went.

I escorted her back to her armchair, pulling a face at Dad which meant 'You talk to her. I need to speak to

Mom,' and rushed into the kitchen where Mom was stacking the dishwasher and muttering furiously (but real quietly!) to herself.

'Mom!' I whispered. 'That old woman stole my stone!'

'She did what?'

'My stone! The one I got in Cardigan—you know.'

'Oh, now honey! Why in the world would she want that?' Mom said, reasonably. 'She wouldn't steal stuff. Not when she's so rich and all.'

'Why not?' I said, fiercely. 'She was snooping in my room when she went to the bathroom. I've got to get a look in her purse, Mom—I *know* she has my stone!'

Mom's face hardened. 'Leave it to me, honey,' she said, and marched into the sitting room.

'Mrs Gwynne-Davies,' she said, brightly. 'I'd love for you to come see my kitchen?'

'Certainly not,' the old lady said. 'Kitchens are for servants.'

Which kind of knocked that idea on the head.

'Would you care to see the garden?' Mom suggested.

'I would not. I have an historical early Elizabethan knot garden on my estate. Also fishponds. Why would I want to look at a back yard?' I looked helplessly at Mom, and shrugged. She gave me a look that said 'I haven't given up yet', but I had a real nasty feeling that Mrs Gwynne-Davies would sail off home with my stone still in her purse.

Nobody noticed Jake trying to escape—not that I could blame him any. He'd gotten as far as the kitchen without anyone spotting him, but when he opened the door to sneak out onto the beach road through the lean-to shed arrangements in back, Madoc, shut in during the visit, shot like a guided missile through the kitchen and into the sitting room, skidding on one of the rag rugs and landing in

78

a heap at my feet. I petted him, laughing despite my missing stone, and was amazed when he growled.

'Madoc!' I said, surprised. He wasn't growling at me, but at Mrs Gwynne-Davies, and if he hadn't been so serious, and hadn't been backing away, kind of brave and scared at the same time, it might have been funny.

The old lady had put her purse on the floor beside her. 'The dog should be trained,' she said. 'Badly-trained animals should be put down.' She scowled, and Madoc growled louder.

'Oh?' Dad said, his voice ominously quiet. 'You think so? Even over here, I think Madoc would have to bite somebody before he got put down. And even then,' he continued, 'it might depend who he bit.' Mom hid a grin behind her hand.

Suddenly, Madoc shot from my restraining hand, rushed across the room, grabbed Mrs Gwynne-Davies's purse and ran out of the room with it. I went after him, through the kitchen and out into the lean-to, where he stopped, turned, and sat waiting patiently for me to take the purse from him.

'Good boy, Madoc!' I snapped the purse open and rummaged inside. A wallet, a cheque book, a lace handkerchief, a tube of extra-strong mints—and right down at the bottom, my stone. The brilliant colours shifted and changed in the dim light of the lean-to. I hid it under a flower-pot on a shelf for safety. Then I gave Madoc a quick kiss, shut the door on him, and tripped back into the sitting room.

'I'm *soooo* sorry, Mrs Gwynne-Davies!' I was having a hard time not grinning. 'I don't know what's gotten into that puppy! Stealing your purse like that! Still and all, here it is, and no harm done!' I handed it back to her. 'I wiped off most of the drool,' I said sweetly. The old lady reached out her gnarled hands and took the purse. She knew the stone had gone, but she couldn't say one word! She scowled, and the hairs in her wart twitched.

'I wish to leave,' she said, angrily, and Dad, looking real happy about that, got her coat.

When she'd gone, I said 'Mom, she did take my stone. But I got it back.'

Mom shook her head. 'Why in the world would she want that, Catrin?'

I fetched the stone from under its flowerpot, and Mom took it from me, turned it over and over in her hands. 'It's a mystery, Catty. It's just a plain old painted rock!'

(Oh no it ain't, Mom, I thought. You just can't see what it really looks like, is all.)

Dad was just as mystified. 'Maybe she's a kleptomaniac. Did you count the teaspoons, honey?' He shrugged. 'I guess we ought to be sorry for her, but she's so darn rude it's kinda hard.'

'What's a klepto-whatyousaid, Dad?' Jake asked, and Dad got the dictionary so Jake could look it up, which Jake hates for him to do, because all he wants is to be told, not to have to look it up in some dumb book, because if you don't spell so good (and Jake doesn't!), what use is a dictionary if you don't even know how a word begins?

'Anyway,' Mom said, collapsing in a heap on the couch. 'I'm real glad that's over! We don't need to ask her again, do we, honey?' she implored.

Dad grinned. 'Oh, maybe just for Thanksgiving, and Christmas, and Easter, and birthdays, and . . .' Mom threw a cushion at him.

The weather stayed fine. Summer seemed to go on forever, and I was outdoors as much as I could be. I wasn't lonely,

80

or bored, like I would have been in Pittsburgh, not with Madoc around. Although he was supposed to be 'our' dog, Jake's and mine, he seemed more and more mine, and followed me everywhere.

One Saturday Mom took him into Cardigan to get some shots at the vet's, but I had chores to do. Mom'd had a tidy-fest, and had decided my room was a dump. Why do Moms get in such a snit about tidyness: I know where everything is, and with the world in such a mess, why should my bedroom be the exception? Just because everything happens to be on the floor rather than put away—well, it's my room, isn't it? Unfortunately, Mom doesn't see it that way.

I tidied it, real fast, by shoving things into drawers and closets, then spent a while polishing my stone and admiring the way the colours shimmered and shifted. At four, I gave up waiting for Mom to come back with Madoc, and went out without him, hating to waste the sunshine altogether. Jake was off with Cei, fishing, and I left a note for Mom propped against the cookie jar so she wouldn't worry any.

There was a brisk offshore breeze that day, with the wind whipping up the incoming tide into rolling surf, the breakers crashing on the beach. I watched a gang of local kids surfing: it looked like fun.

I took off my sneakers and waded along the tideline, enjoying the water sluicing across my feet and the cold, silky sand between my toes. The beach was almost empty, apart from the surfers. I loved the solitude, the gulls wheeling and screaming. I screamed back at them, startling them away. A hand fell on my shoulder.

'Hello, Catrin.'

I jumped. 'Oh, hi, Twm.'

We walked in silence for a while. I was kind of embarrassed, getting caught talking back at gulls, so I said 'No sign of anything weird happening yet, Twm!' in a teasing kind of way. Then I wished I hadn't.

Twm went red. 'Don't poke fun, Catrin. It isn't a joke. It *will* come, and then you will see. Why was the old woman at your house?'

'Old woman? Have you been spying on us?'

He shook his head. 'Of course not. Where that woman goes, I know about it.'

'She came for tea,' I said, frowning. 'Actually, she kind of invited herself: she told Dad she was coming, and Dad just kind of went along with it.'

'When she came,' Twm said, urgently, 'think: how many times did your Mam ask her to come in?'

I tried to remember. 'Sheesh, Twm! I can't recall! No. Wait a minute'. I screwed up my face, trying to remember. 'Yeah. Just the one time.'

Twm's brow cleared, and his weird, pale eyes were relieved.

'Good. But don't forget, Catrin,' he reminded me, 'take care. You must be careful who you invite in—'

'Who-I-invite-in-my-house-three-times,' I finished for him. 'Yeah, yeah, Twm. I'll be careful, I promise. But this strange happening of yours is taking one heck of a time to get here. I'm getting kind of tired of waiting!'

'Don't poke fun, Catrin,' he said again. 'Just—take care.'

CHAPTER SEVEN

I bought a surfboard a couple of days later, and immediately wondered why I couldn't surf when surfers made it look so easy! I paddled like crazy, but the waves just carried right on up the beach and left me behind, bobbing in the green water. Any waves I caught were mostly luck, I guess, because I didn't do it often. I swim real good, but surfing's hard! I'd tried all day, until the sun was about to go down. By then I was a real pretty shade of blue, with chattering teeth, and decided it was time to go home. Jake was off having tea with Cei, and Twm had promised to bring him back later.

'Hi Mom!' I hollered, dumping my sandy board and wet swimsuit in the outhouse and opening the kitchen door.

'Shhh!' she said, putting her finger to her lips.

'Why?'

'Mrs Gwynne-Davies is here! She just came, and I can't get rid of her! I've tried dropping hints to get her to go, but she just sits there like a frog on a log.'

'Oh, great,' I said. 'Did she go upstairs at all?'

'No, she didn't. She's in the sitting room. Go see her.'

I groaned. 'Aw, Mom! Do I have to? Can't I sneak upstairs? I don't like her, Mom.'

'Go be polite, *please* honey?'

I sighed. 'Just for you, Mom. Can we have fish fingers for supper?'

'Tomorrow. Tonight I'm having to make company-type tea. She seems to have invited herself again.'

When Dad was home, we ate tea in the dining room, not off trays on our laps watching TV. Mrs Gwynne-Davies ate and ate, greedy as a hog, but each time I looked up, she was watching me. Chewing, stuffing her face with goodies, but watching me.

After, she asked to go upstairs again. She insisted she could go alone, but as soon as I heard the bathroom door close, I shot upstairs and hid my stone egg. Madoc might not be able to get it back a second time. I slipped it in my underwear drawer, then sat on the bed to wait for her to go downstairs again. I wasn't taking any chances! She came out of the bathroom, and sure enough, her warty old face soon appeared round the door.

'Hi, Mrs Gwynne-Davies!' I said sweetly, 'Can I help you with anything? Towel, maybe?' After her last visit Mom found her towel draped over a rosebush under the bathroom window.

'No,' she said, her eyes narrowing. 'Nothing. But I know who you are, girl, make no mistake about that!'

Excuse me? Oh, boy, she was majorly, majorly nuts! I shivered, hoping she'd go home before she went *completely* bananas.

At six o'clock, Twm arrived with Jake and Cei. Their faces were rosy from the wind, and they brought the cold smell of the night sea to the door with them.

'Come in, Twm, Cei,' Mom invited. Cei and Jake shot upstairs to Jake's room, and Twm—on the first asking!—stepped inside, smiling.

'I guess you know Mrs Gwynne-Davies?' Mom asked. Twm just stared, his strange, light eyes fixed on the old lady, his face like stone.

'Cei,' Twm called, urgently. 'Come now, please.'

Bewildered, Cei scurried downstairs and Twm grabbed his hand, dragging him out the door. Mom looked mystified. I followed them out, closing the door behind me, and wrapping my arms round me for warmth. The days were real hot, but there was a chill night wind off the sea.

'What was all that about?' I asked. 'Kind of rude, weren't you? She's only an old lady. A real rude old lady, sure, but, Twm!'

'Oh, Catrin,' Twm whispered. 'That woman—she is—she . . .' he stammered, then stopped.

'Is she who—? The thing you've been warning me about?' I asked, suddenly excited and nervous all at once.

'No. But she's part of it. She's powerful. Watch her. Be careful. It's you she wants.'

'Me?' I squeaked. 'Like, aah—me, myself, personally?'

'Or something you have. Think, now. You must have found one of the Signs already, and aren't aware of it. So, what?'

It had to be the stone egg. She'd stolen it once already. 'She seems kinda keen to get hold of my pebble, Twm. Could that be one of the signs?'

Twm frowned. 'I don't know. Can't tell unless I see it. But if she wants it . . .'

'Shall I go fetch it?' I offered. He shook his head.

'No. Not now, not with a Spoiler there. I'll see it another time: then I'll know.'

Spoiler? 'Oh, fooph,' I said, scowling. 'I wish you'd quit talking in circles, Twm. I can't understand half of what you say!'

Twm collected Cei from half way up an apple tree, and left. By the time I reached the front door and turned to wave after him, he had disappeared into the twilight.

In the sitting room, Dad's face was thunderous, and Mom was biting her lip.

'I don't like that boy,' Mrs Gwynne-Davies said. 'He is

rude and unpleasant. Not suitable for your daughter. I am shocked that you allow her to speak to him.'

There she goes again, I thought! Calling me a child.

'I like him,' Dad said firmly. 'He's a pleasant young man and his manners are impeccable. He can come by any time he wants.'

'Thanks, Dad!' I said, grinning, and he knew I didn't just mean thanks for letting Twm come over any time, but thanks for sticking up for him with the old witch.

No sooner had the word crossed my mind than I found myself staring at her. And she was staring back at me, with a look on her face that said she knew what I was thinking. She did look exactly like a witch! She was ugly, had a hooked nose, and hairy warts—and she was certainly unpleasant enough!

The crash of the dragon's head doorknocker startled us all—I squeaked and shot about six inches in the air with fright. Dad opened it, and grinned with relief when he saw the uniformed chauffeur outside, waiting for Mrs Gwynne-Davies.

'Wait in the car, Humphreys,' the old lady ordered. 'I shall be out directly.' The man nodded and went back to the car.

And then time stood still.

She began to whirl, faster and faster, until she became a shadowy, blurred shape, like a spinning top. Mom and Dad, and Jake, who had come in from the kitchen with his face stuffed full of cookie, were moving in slow motion, like, like—they were on video and the person with the zapper was moving them forward one frame at a time, y'know? Only Mrs Gwynne-Davies and I were moving normally—well, *I* was. She was a mass of spinning darkness. Suddenly she stopped still and glared at me.

'I know you, Miss!' she said. 'I want the Egg. The other Signs I shall have, but I want the Egg. Make no mistake: when I have it, and the other Signs, then you and boy will suffer. Now, fetch me the stone at once.'

'I don't know what you're talking about,' I said, and was amazed my voice was completely calm. 'You can't have the stone, it's mine. I don't know about any other things, but I do know about the stone egg. You're nuts if you think I'm gonna give it to you! And please, don't threaten us. We aren't afraid of you.'

The old lady's eyes glittered. 'Then you should be, you stupid child. The longer you delay, the worse it will be for you. Fetch the stone, now.'

I was beginning to get frightened. 'No!' I squeaked. 'You can't have it.' She drew back her right arm, her hand clenched—not like she was gonna *hit* me, but like she was gonna throw something at me!

Suddenly the door burst open and Madoc, a small whirlwind of fury, helter-skeltered in and flung himself at the back of the old lady's knees. She lurched, stumbled, and something small fell out of her hand, landing fizzing on one of Mom's rag rugs, which burst into brilliant blue crackling flames. Almost as if Madoc's attack had broken the old woman's concentration, Mom, Dad and Jake started moving again.

'Good gravy!' Mom yelped, staring aghast at the blazing rug. 'How on earth did that happen?'

Dad picked up the almost completely burned rug by one corner, (yay for tiled floors—a carpet would have burned too) and tossed it into the hearth, where it fizzled out harmlessly. Meantime, unnoticed, Mrs Gwynne-Davies left. The headlights of her car swept across the ceiling as her driver reversed away from the garden gate.

Dad scratched his head. 'Spontaneous combustion!' he said. 'No fire to throw sparks, no smokers in this house, no Jake playing with matches.' (Jake scowled: he'd almost up burned his bedroom once when he was a little kid, and Dad had never let him forget it.) 'How did that happen?' Dad shook his head, amazed.

I opened my mouth to explain that Mrs Gwynnne-Davies had been about to throw a spell at me, and if it hadn't been for Madoc, who made her drop it, it might have been us barbecued, not the rag rug, and . . . Then I shut it again. Nah. Sure they'd believe me. Not.

Dad's hair was sticking up in spikes where he'd ruffled it trying to keep his cool. Mom reached up to smoothe it down. 'Never mind, honey,' she soothed. 'Maybe a match-head broke off and lodged in the fabric one time, and somebody trod on it and the rug caught fire.'

Sure, Mom, I thought. Only you've forgotten that all the rugs were washed before they were put down, and shampooed match-heads certainly do not catch fire.

I recalled my conversation with Twm. Even though everyone else saw just a painted stone egg, I saw different. I saw 'beautiful' and 'magical', and I just knew Twm would see it that way, too. There didn't seem much doubt. My stone egg had to be the Sign. I couldn't wait to show it to Twm!

CHAPTER EIGHT

Later, I took the stone from my underwear drawer and hid it in my closet with the candy box I'd planned to keep all Kym's letters in. The ones I didn't get any of yet. It was kinda weird, though. Kym didn't seem so important, now. So much was happening here in the back end of nowhere that I hardly thought about Pittsburgh. I turned the key of the closet and hung it round my neck on a chain I never took off, so I knew it would be safe. And the Troll might make it up to my room, but she couldn't get into my closet without the key.

In the kitchen Jake, his walkman headphones clamped to his ears, a comic book propped on the milk jug, was chomping his way through a bowl of cocopops before calling for Cei. Mom, armed with her antiques guide, had headed for some country house sale in the next county. I reached for the cornflakes and poured out a bowl, chopped a banana and sloshed creamy milk on top—my favourite breakfast after waffles and honey, which is totally ace, but for special occasions only, because according to Mom it's tooth decay in a dish. After, I cleared away and loaded the dishwasher while Jake put the cereals and milk away.

'Jake,' I said, before heading for the beach, 'will you ask Twm to meet me in the dunes at two today, please?'

Jake pulled a face. 'Wow, Catrin's sweet on Twm! Catty's got a boyfriend, Catty's got a boyfriend, Catty's got a . . .'

I put him in a headlock and knuckled his head until he hollered quit, which was something I have to do occasionally, just to keep him in line. 'Cut it out, Jake. He's just my friend. So just do it, Jake, OK? Or—you're hamburger!'

I must still be able to terrify him even though he's almost as tough as me these days, because Twm was waiting for me at two, sitting on a dune chewing a bit of rough grass, his legs brown and bare in washed-out denim shorts.

Light, powdery sand slithered under my sneakers as I sat beside him. Madoc licked his hand and sat patiently at my feet, his curious eyes moving from Twm's face to mine. Twm's welcoming grin disappeared when I explained what had happened.

'She kinda paralysed everyone but me. I don't know what would have happened if Madoc hadn't knocked her off balance.' The puppy shifted slightly at the sound of his name, his tail thumping sand. 'The rug just burned right up, Twm! It's the stone egg she wants. It *has* to be the sign!'

'Did you bring it with you?' he asked.

'No. I hid it. If she sneaks in the house while I'm away, I don't want her to find my egg. She can turn everybody slo-mo, like they were walking in molasses or something, so I guess she can probably look through walls too. But she's not gonna get my egg. No way!' I finished, fiercely.

Twm nodded, slowly. 'I tried to warn you, Catrin. If she can alter time and space—what you call "slo-mo"—that's Yankspeak for "slow motion", is it?' I nodded.

'Then someone invited her three times before she entered your home . . .' He let his voice tail off. 'I think it's time you met my Taid, Catrin.'

'Your Grandfather? Mrs Pugh said he was related to Merlin. Just kidding, I guess!' I added real fast, not wanting him to think we'd been gossiping about him.

He grinned, his teeth white against his tan. 'No, she wasn't, Catrin. If anyone's related to Merlin my Taid is. Wait and see. Come tomorrow. Bring the stone egg.'

Of course, next day I had to tell Mom where I was going, and of course Mom insisted on making up a basket of goodies for me to bring. I felt like Little Red Riding Hood by the time I got out, with a wicker basket stuffed full of fudge brownies, apple pie and peanut cookies. I guess my Mom is a cookoholic. I hid the stone under the food at the bottom of the basket.

I met Twm on the bridge leading into Pontpentre-dŵr village. I got there first, and amused myself playing Poohsticks, dropping bits of twig off one side of the bridge and betting with myself which bit would go faster. I was so engrossed with the race between a twig with a dead leaf attached, and another twig without, I didn't hear him coming. The dead leaf acted like a sail, because it was miles ahead of the other one.

'What's in the basket, Catrin?' Twm asked.

'Sheesh, Twm, you scared me half to death!' I protested. Some cookies and stuff, that's all. And the stone egg, of course.'

We set off towards the village, almost a mile away along the leafy lane. Twm's grandfather's cottage was a tiny, white-washed place with huge boulders at the bottom for foundations, and smaller stones making the walls. It was square, like a dollhouse, with two windows on top and two at the bottom, and a green-painted wooden door planted dead in the middle, framed and draped in rambling roses. The top half of the stable door was wide open onto the garden, which was arched with sweet-smelling honeysuckle, loud with bees and starry with cream and yellow flowers. The garden path, like *Mary, Mary*'s, was edged with seashells. Hollyhocks and sunflowers towered, and the mingled scents of a hundred different blossoms made me feel tipsy. Twm opened the front door, and I followed him inside, my eyes not working after the sunshine outside. When my eyes adjusted, I said, 'Aw, Twm. Looks like nobody's home.'

'Look again, Catrin.' I did, and to my amazement, sitting beside the black iron fireplace right in front of me, in a high-backed carved wooden chair, was an old man. I'm sure he wasn't there before! His eyes were a brighter blue than Twm's, and his hair, fine and white, stood out like a dandelion clock. His long, silver beard trailed down his chest. I'd half-expected him to be wearing a black robe spangled with stars and stuff, but he was dressed real ordinary old guy style, in dark trousers, white collarless shirt with the sleeves rolled up over thin brown arms, and a gold watch-chain looped across the front of his black waistcoat. He spoke rapidly to Twm in Welsh, and Twm replied, smiling. I tried not to stare, but it was kind of hard. The old man put out his hand for me to shake, and I took it. His face was kind and wise.

'So you are Catrin!' he said. 'Twm has told me all about you. *Croeso, ferch.*'

I smiled. 'Twm spends most of his time getting on my case over something or other. I hope he didn't tell you all the dumb things I do.'

'Well, I don't know. There's a bully you are, Twm.' He patted my hand before letting go. 'He hasn't told me anything bad about you, not at all. It isn't often we get foreigners round here, you know!' he said.

The words were out of my mouth before I had time to think. 'I am not either a foreigner!' I retorted indignantly. 'I'm half Welsh! My Dad is a son of Wales, Mr Pugh said.' Then I wished I could call the words back. I couldn't believe I'd said it! Of course I was a foreigner. I'd lived mostly my whole life in Pittsburgh, Pennsylvania. But deep down inside I knew that the Welsh half of me had taken over the American half. I loved this place, and my roots were sinking into the rich soil of Wales. 'Omigosh, I'm so sorry!' I said. I knew my face was scarlet.

But the old man smiled. 'She'll do, Twm. She'll do.'

He reached out and pulled me towards him to sit on a small stool at his knee. 'Now, tell me all about it. You first, Twm.'

'I told you I had warnings, Taid,' Twm began. 'About the Estuary and the Bay, but I can't see what the danger is, or how it will come. The old woman . . .'

'Mrs Gwynne-Davies,' I interrupted.

'. . . she's already got into the Toll House—she was asked three times, Catrin's Mam not knowing, you see. She is a Spoiler, Taid, and knows me for a Defender.'

The old man nodded soberly. 'How did you know her, Twm?'

Twm shook his head. 'I don't know. There is something about her, Taid, a mist, a smell of otherness. She could not meet my eyes.'

I was, like, totally lost. Spoilers? Otherness?

Twm's grandfather took my hand and squeezed it as if he'd read my mind. 'The Spoilers are those who work against us, Catrin. When countryside is torn up and a factory built which pollutes the streams, the rivers, the sea, Spoilers are behind it. When oil drenches a seashore and thousands of wild creatures die, smothered in sticky black, the Spoilers are there, delaying, distracting, hindering—spoiling. The Defenders guard the magic of the earth and sky and sea, and try to keep them whole and pure. The Spoilers work against us: the more damage they can do to the earth, the more poison they can flood into the land, the more powerful they become. Our way, if you like, is summer; theirs is eternal, bitter winter.'

I gulped. Was this for real? Again, he sensed my doubts.

'I know, child. I understand how strange all this must sound, especially to a child of the New World. But here, Otherness is very close. You will understand, I promise.' He smiled. 'But enough of this gloomy talk, Twm. We're frightening Catrin. Tell me, cariad. What is in your basket?'

Lifting it on my knees, I took out the stone in its box and set it aside, thinking he meant Mom's goodies. 'Brownies,' I said, 'and apple pie, and—'

'And what is this?' the old man asked, picking up the box containing the stone.

Putting the basket down again, I took the box from him and took out the stone egg. Before I unwrapped it, I paused.

'The thing is,' I began, 'when I look at this I see one thing. When other guys look, they see something else. My Mom and Dad and Jake, they see just an old painted stone. I don't. Trouble is, I don't know whether *they're* nuts—or I am!'

Taid took the package from me and unwrapped it, placing the shimmering object on his wrinkled palm. Sky-blue, turquoise, lapis lazuli, azure, gentian, ice, more blues than were possible swirled and changed, gleaming softly in the dark cottage kitchen. His face was expressionless.

'So, now. Tell me, Catrin. What do you see?'

I sighed. He couldn't see it. How could I describe it to someone who might as well be blind? It's like when you're asked what something tastes like: how can you describe it? They have to taste it for themselves, don't they? I looked at

Twm for help, but his face was blank as a sheet of paper waiting for a story. I tried, anyhow.

I took a deep breath. 'It's an oval stone, about twice the size of a chicken egg, and heavy. It's coloured, but it is not painted, no matter what anyone says. The colours swirl and move and shimmer and the blueness of it is all the blues you can think of: skies, seas, bluebells, hyacinths, forget-me-nots—all of those and a million more besides. The stone is opaque, but it seems like you ought to be able to see into it, even if you can't see through it. You only know that the deepness is there.' I sighed. 'I guess that's the best I can do. And I still can't describe it well enough for you to see what it's like if you can't see it for yourself. If you only see a painted stone . . .' I quit. Either they saw it, or they didn't.

Taid turned his hand so that the stone shimmered. 'Trust me, Catrin,' he said softly. 'Twm and I see exactly what you see. This is the Sky Egg. Twm is right. It is the first Sign.'

'You see it?' I gasped 'Really? You're not puttin' me on?'

Twm snorted with laughter. 'We're not putting you on, Catrin.' He squatted down so his eyes were on a level with Taid's hand, and the stone. 'It's the most beautiful thing I've seen in my whole life,' he said, softly. 'And if you have it, then you are the Girl.'

'I am?' I said uncertainly. 'What girl?'

Taid lowered the Sky Egg back into its box, nested in the silky fabric it had been wrapped in.

'There are three legends,' he began . . .

So if you skipped the legends, you need to read them NOW!

CHAPTER NINE

When I'd heard the three Legends, I was entranced, hardly daring to move.

'Hey, wait up,' I said, suddenly realising. 'Are you telling me this is the Sky Egg?' Taid nodded.

'So how come I got it? If that guy—what was his name, Taliesin?—buried it at the crossroads, how could I pick it up in Cardigan Market? Aw, you're winding me up!'

Taid picked up my empty mug of tea and handed it to Twm to take outside. I didn't remember drinking it, and the number of fudge brownies had gone down, too.

'We aren't, I promise, Catrin. There's a reason why you've got the Sky Egg. Haven't you guessed yet?'

I shook my head. I mean, what? Some old legends, yeah? Drowned cities? Magical harps? Disappearing houses?

'Catrin,' Taid said, and he took my hands between his, brown-spotted and wrinkled with age. 'Catrin, *cariad*. You have the Sky Egg because you are the Sea-Girl.'

I pulled my hands away, scared now. 'You're nuts!' I cried. 'I'm Catrin Rhys Morgan, of Pittsburgh, Pennsylvania. I'm not a legend! I'm me!'

Twm laughed. 'Of course you are, Catrin. But you say you are Welsh, too!'

I opened my mouth to deny it, to say that Wales was just a fold in time. But I couldn't. I had felt such a sense of home-coming. Didn't the sea pull me towards it from the moment I arrived? I'd stopped feeling American after the first week. I was home, and I couldn't deny it. There was something about this land that something in me longed for.

But was I the Sea-Girl?

'Yes,' I admitted. 'I guess I do feel at home. I love Wales. But how can I be the Sea-Girl? I'm still me!'

Taid smiled. 'We don't know for certain if you are the Sea-Girl. I am almost sure—but if the other two Signs come to you, we will know.'

'And if I get the Sea-Harp and the Earthstone, then what? What do I do with them?'

'That we don't know, Catrin, not yet.' Taid said. 'But don't worry about it. If they come, they come. But since you have the Sky Egg—then I think that the other Signs will follow.'

'But what do they look like? How will I recognise them? Where shall I look?'

Taid laughed. 'They will find you, I expect. The Sky Egg did, didn't it?'

'But how did the Sky Egg get into that little back room in the market?' I asked, twisting the shimmering stone.

'Catrin,' Twm said patiently, like he was talking to a halfwit, 'there *are* no back rooms in Cardigan Market.'

'There are so! I got the Sky Egg and my Mom got her writing desk there.'

'You did indeed. I have seen the desk myself. But the room you described does not exist.'

I wrapped the Sky Egg back up in its cloth. 'Of course the room is there,' I said, crossly. 'Taid, will you take care of this for me please?'

Taid shook his head. 'No, Catrin. The Sky Egg has been entrusted to you, and you must keep it. When you find the other Signs, we will know. If you don't find them, then that is just a pretty stone. But beware of Mrs Gwynne-Davies, and others like her who know now that you have the Egg. Take care, Catrin.'

Twm walked me home as far as the bridge, and then

walked upriver to find Jake and Cei. I carried the Sky Egg in the wicker basket, and once Twm left me, spent most of the time looking over my shoulder in case someone was lurking behind a bush waiting to pounce on me! But I got home safely, and, dumping the empty wicker basket in the kitchen, took the Sky Egg upstairs, and opened my closet to hide it. Then I shut it again. That was kind of an obvious place. I examined the lock, and jerked it against the catch. It was not strong. Someone with a knife, or even a credit card, something like that, could get inside real easy. I racked my brains, turning slowly in the centre of the floor, searching for a better hiding place. My eye fell on my four-post bed, and I dragged a chair over and stood on it. With the extra height, I could just see into the fabric canopy draped over the top, and I popped the box into the dip. Then I got on the bed, lay on my back and looked up. I could just make out the square box-shape outlined in the floral fabric. It was safe. No one would find it there unless they got in bed or stood on a chair!

Next Saturday, I got Mom to take me to Cardigan Market. While she trotted off to Tesco, I went to look for the tiny, dark room crammed with old books and sheet music, wind-up gramophones and large black records—and the bent old guy in charge. The whitewashed basement was cool and airy, and the corner where the shop should have been was no different to the other corners. There was no room, no shop. I got some real funny looks from the stallholders when I got to rapping on the walls. I skinned my knuckles. The antique shop did not exist. When I met Mom at the entrance to the market I insisted she came back inside with me.

'Mom,' I said. 'You remember the little place with the old guy, where you bought your writing desk?'

Mom looked at me blankly. 'My escritoire? Sure, why?'

I led her round the corner of a bookstall and pointed out the place where the shop should have been. 'So where is it?' I asked.

Mom looked at the blank corner, and looked at me. Her face was worried. Aha! I thought.

'Cat, honey,' she said, feeling my forehead the way she does when I get sick. 'Are you feeling OK?'

I jerked my head away from her hand. 'Sure I am. I'm fine. So where's the shop, Mom, and the old Man?'

Mom looked distracted. 'Well, I'm sure I don't know. Maybe the old man just isn't here today. Anyhow, honey, I don't recall any little room. It was just a stall, set out like it has been today—just behind you.'

My mouth fell open. I looked at the stall, which had old china stuff on it, and was tended by a fat lady with bleached-blonde hair. 'But . . .' I began, and then closed my mouth. Mom turned round and marched straight to the drugstore where she bought some aspirin.

On the way home in the car, I came to a conclusion. Like it or not, I, Catrin Rhys Morgan, formerly of Pittsburgh, Pennsylvania, United States of America, was beginning to believe in magic. Omigosh. Kymmburleigh would think I was totally insane.

CHAPTER TEN

Next day was kind of grey, and too cold to swim, so I took Madoc and walked miles along the shoreline, thinking. We were racing against the incoming tide on the way back—hurrying, so we wouldn't get cut off, icy foam licking my ankles, Madoc dancing in and out of the waves like a mad thing. I rubbed most of the sand off him in the outhouse before letting him inside. He thought this was real keen: my face got washed every time it came within licking range.

Mom was stringing beans at the kitchen table, and I could smell Dad's favourite pot roast. So could Madoc, because he took up guard duty right next the Aga.

'Need any help, Mom?'

'No, honey, thanks. I'm about all set once I'm done with these beans. Oh, a letter came for you.'

'A letter! Who from?'

'It's on the dresser.'

A blue airmail envelope was propped against a cracked willow-pattern pitcher that, back home, Mom would have chucked—but I guess the cracks were antique.

Kym had written! The envelope seemed kind of thin. When I opened it I wasn't sure whether I was sad or angry or what. She'd hardly managed to write me one single page! No news of the guys back home, no gossip—it was like she was writing to a stranger. She didn't answer any of my questions, she didn't give me any news, didn't ask if I was homesick, didn't even say she was missing me. Some best buddy! And she was gonna 'just die' when I left. Yeah, sure, Kym. Crossly I crumpled the thin blue sheet and tossed it in the waste-basket. She was supposed to be my best friend. Maybe Mom was right—Kym didn't really care much for me at all. Mom glanced up sympathetically.

'Disappointed, sweetheart?'

I nodded. I felt kind of snuffly. 'We were gonna be best friends even if we weren't gonna see each other. Her letter was, like, one big zero, Mom! No news, no gossip, nothing. She didn't even try to write me, and I wrote pages and pages to her!'

'Well, honey, at least you've got Twm. And when you start school you'll make scads more new buddies, I'm sure. There's banana cream pie for dessert. Cheer up.'

Good old Mom. Food was the answer to everything. If my life ever got real tragic, I'd probably end up weighing three hundred pounds and have to stay home because I couldn't get through the doors!

'I guess I'll get over it, Mom. But I don't think I'm gonna write Kym again until she writes me a good long letter with lots and lots of news.' I decided it was time to change the subject. 'Hey, Mom. How come you haven't been antique hunting lately? Must be at least a week! Is the Enthusiasm beginning to wear off!'

'Oh, you!' she said, mock-crossly. Then she said, 'Yes, I guess it is. I've gotten some lovely pieces, but they cost a whole lot, and we don't have room for much more, not if we want to live here too. But you know, Catty, kind of weird you should ask. I met this real nice lady in a coffee shop downtown today, and she belongs to this writers' group. So I've decided to join—I've always written bits and bobs of poetry and stuff, and it'd be real good to do some writing over here. I could do an anthology of writing about Wales.' She propped her chin on her hand. 'Can you think of a rhyme for Pontpentre-dŵr?'

I almost choked. Mom, writing poetry? 'Not off hand,' I

said, trying not to grin. Well, at least the new Enthusiasm wouldn't be noisy, or expensive, and best of all, we wouldn't have to eat, drink, or wear the results!

At dinner, Mom told Dad all about it. Jake grinned at me, and Dad mumbled through his pot roast.

'Sounds good, honey,' he said. 'Where d'they hold the meetings?'

'Now isn't that just the oddest thing?' Mom said, happily spooning green beans onto Jake's plate. He hates them. 'They don't have a meeting place—they meet in each others' homes. It'll be a real good chance for me to meet the natives. Next Tuesday it's at a Mrs Evans' place, in Aberaeron, and the week after I've invited them all here!'

I had a sudden thought. 'Does Mrs Gwynne-Davies have anything to do with this, Mom?'

Mom shook her head, and rapped Jake's knuckles with her serving spoon to stop him slipping the green beans under the table to Madoc, who wasn't supposed to be there. 'No. But strange you should say that, because Mr Humphreys, her chauffeur, does!'

'Hey Mom,' I said, thinking about Humphreys, and the Troll, 'd'you mind if I stick around? It sounds like it might be keen. I could help pass round the coffee and stuff if you want.'

Mom beamed. 'Sure you can, Catty! You can never have too much exposure to culture, honey, never too much culture. You kids nowadays don't read poetry for pleasure the way I used to when I was your age. And Wales sets great store by its poets, isn't that right, David?'

Dad was looking at me suspiciously. I grinned. 'I'm interested in learning about writing, OK Dad? You never know, I might decide to be a writer some day.'

'Hmph,' Dad said.

I couldn't explain that I needed to stick around just in case Humphreys was one of Them. After the blazing rug, I didn't want to be out that evening and come home and find the Toll House burned to the ground and my Mom barbecued!

After dinner, Twm rang, asking if I wanted to go out in his boat next day. 'The weather forecast is good, and the tide will be right to land on the island. If you'd like to come, we could spend the day there.'

Do monkeys climb trees? 'Oh, wow, Twm! That'd be just great. Let me just check with Mom.' I tucked the phone into my chest and hollered 'Mom! Can I go with Twm in the boat tomorrow? Over to the island?'

Mom and Dad had a muttered conversation. Then Dad said 'Sure, honey.'

They obviously trusted Twm—and his seamanship.

I put the phone back to my ear again. 'Yeah, Twm. I'm allowed.'

'Should I bring a picnic?'

'No. Taid and I will do one. We were eating your Mam's cooking for days after you came. Taid said your father must be big as a mountain.'

I chuckled. 'I guess he will be, soon. Back home, Dad used to jog every day, but here—well, I guess sometime he'll need to diet.'

'I heard that,' Dad said crossly. 'I am not getting fat—my trousers have shrunk, is all.'

'Hah!' Mom said.

Although she'd already said I could go, naturally, next day Mom kicked up a Mom-type fuss. She insisted I had to wear a life-preserver, I was not allowed to swim unless Twm said the currents were OK, I wasn't to take any risks

103

at all and I had to be back by dark. I had to dress real warm even though it was at least eighty in the shade. When she finally ran out of must-do's and don't dare's, I grabbed my sweater and ran to meet Twm at the bridge. He wore denim cut-offs and a T-shirt, but had a heavy navy wool sweater slung over the top of a bulging rucksack.

We walked down to the tiny cove just around the jagged point of rocks at the southern end of 'our' bay, and I helped him drag the dinghy to the water's edge and launch it, splashing thigh-deep in the clear, cold sea. Once aboard I sat excitedly gripping the blue-painted sides of the boat while Twm started up the outboard, and soon we were puttering over a gentle swell towards the island rising like a green lizard from the ocean.

I trailed my fingers, watching the water foam white away from my hand, the sun making rainbows in the droplets. It was real hot: even far out in the bay there was so little wind it was hardly any cooler.

The island was further away than it looked. It took us almost half an hour to reach it and travel round to the seaward side, facing out into Cardigan Bay and Ireland, out of sight of the mainland. A small, sandy cove curved into the shore, and a stone jetty was built onto the rocks, jutting out to sea, with strands of green and black seaweed all around it rising and falling with the swell of the tide. Steps had been cut into the rocks, climbing steeply upwards. The cove was in shadow, because the sun wasn't high yet, but later the sand would probably be hot enough to burn our feet. I expected Twm to putter up to the jetty, but instead he cut the engine and the boat stopped, rocking gently in the swell. He dropped an anchor—a big stone with a rope threaded through a hole, to stop the pull of the tide washing us out to sea or onto the rocks. The water was like blue glass streaked with emerald and sapphire, and the rocky walls rising above us were alive with birds, completely un-bothered by us.

Gulls wheeled and screamed at the top of the cliff, cormorants posed like Chinese paintings on the rocks, their black necks curved; guillemots floated in living, dark brown rafts all round us, and clown-faced puffins bobbed and craned to see us. All around the boat flew the graceful shearwaters, stiff-winged, dark upper bodies and glimpses of pale undersides as they skimmed the glowing surface of the sea and soared above our heads. I was so fascinated by the sky-dancers that I didn't notice the dark heads silently lifting out of the water all around.

Twm cleared his throat softly, calling my attention to the intelligent dark eyes of at least a dozen grey seals solemnly inspecting us.

'Ssssh, Catrin,' he whispered. 'Don't make any sudden movements.'

I did as I was bid, hardly breathing, captivated by the animals' intent and interested gaze. Who was watching whom? Twm peeled off his T-shirt and dived cleanly over the side, and instantly the seals disappeared. Gazing down into the clear water I saw streamlined black shapes surrounding Twm's golden body, twisting and turning around him. Twm stayed underwater far longer than I thought possible, catching rides from willing flippers, tumbling over and over, weightless, as perfectly at home in the water as the seals. I was beginning to worry that he might drown, when he swam up beside the boat, his sun-streaked hair dark and wet, sleek as the seals bobbing up around him.

He heaved himself back on board, hauled up the anchor, started the engine again and steered the boat carefully in towards the tiny jetty where he tied up to a huge iron ring.

'Does anyone live here, Twm?' I asked, puffing up the steep steps, coarse grass scratching my bare ankles. He stopped at the top and reached down a hand to heave me up the final steep step.

'Not any more. There were people here until the war, but they left, then, and never came back. I expect they got used to living in cities and couldn't face being all alone back on the island, after. The wild creatures have it again, now.'

A little way back from the cliff, in a sun-filled hollow, was an old house, its door hanging from rusted hinges, window frames empty except for twining brambles. The roof was turf on which wildflowers had seeded themselves until it was quite overgrown, so that the house seemed to be wearing a fine head of long hair, blowing in the sea-breeze. We ate in the sweet-smelling, run-wild cottage garden, sheltered by dry stone walls.

Taid had made a wonderful picnic, full of home baking: pasties, cookies, and fruity *bara brith*, and when we were finished and full to bursting we lay fatly for a while in the hollow beside the house, dozing. Later, Twm prodded me in the ribs. 'Come on, idleness,' he said. 'I'll show you my Island.'

It was beautiful, although in winter it would be a bleak place. Twm showed me curious rings of mossy stone set in the coarse sea-grass—the remains, he said, of stone age dwellings. We drank from the island's water supply, an icy spring bubbling up from an outcrop of rocks, flowing down beside the house, disappearing again on the far side of the hollow. He showed me darker green marks on the turf, perfect circles of wildflowers, and neat rings of coloured pebbles.

'*Tylwyth Teg*,' he said, in explanation. Now if some guy

back home had shown me flowery circles in the grass and told me they were fairy rings, I'd have lit out for home, hollering for the guys in white coats, but here—it didn't seem so weird, y'know? Then, the sun began its slow stoop towards the horizon, and it was time to leave the island to the wild things.

CHAPTER ELEVEN

We collected Twm's rucksack and scrambled down the cliff steps. Although we went real easy, sitting birds were still startled into flight, and small animals scuttled and rustled in the long grass. My face stung with sun and salt, and if I lived to be a hundred and fifty I'd never have such a day again.

But it wasn't over yet. Twm jumped into the boat and reached up to help me in. He prodded the boat away from the jetty with the end of his oar, but didn't start the outboard immediately, rowing out a little way instead.

'Close your eyes,' he ordered. The sun was red against the inside of my eyelids. I heard an odd, thudding splash and recognised the sound as Twm's hand, slapping the surface of the sea. I couldn't work out why, though.

'Open your eyes, Catrin.'

I opened them—and ducked: a huge, silvery-blue and dark grey body rose over us, and for a second I was scared. I needn't have worried—the dolphin arched, and slid into the water with barely a splash.

A little way off, a dorsal fin and a smooth flank broke the water, and then another and another, until suddenly we were surrounded by dolphins. Twm, leaning over the bow, patted gleaming heads and flanks, and they nuzzled his hands, chirping and whistling, and Twm whistled back, communicating. Twm, listening, suddenly lost his smile. And then the dolphins were gone as swiftly as they had appeared, arching and knifing through the water out into the vastness of Cardigan Bay.

'What's wrong, Twm?' I asked. His face was bleak.

'The Sea-People are warning me, Catrin. There will be danger. Soon. And we only have the one Sign.'

I shivered despite the heat. I didn't want to know about Signs, or danger. I wanted to dream of seals, birds, dolphins, enchanted islands and wild beauty.

We slid inshore on the tide, Twm silent and preoccupied.

Back home, the first thing I did was check that the Sky Egg was still safely in its hiding place. I crawled onto the bed and looked up, seeing the angular shape of the box outlined in the canopy. It was still there.

That night, I dreamed of dolphins.

Mom's poetry evening arrived, and from early morning she was rattling round the kitchen baking stuff and getting herself, like, totally wound up. Jake had no intention of being anywhere he was gonna run into poems, and had wangled an invitation to tea with Cei.

Dad, judging by his expression at breakfast when Mom reminded him about it, thought he might be real late home from the office. So it was just Mom and me.

The first to arrive was a lady from the village, Mrs Prosser. She was through the door almost before I had it open, and her beady little eyes took in every detail of the living room and stored it all away. She plonked herself fatly down on the sofa and talked at us. She didn't wait for answers—she just kept right on yattering.

Next came two twittering elderly ladies: sisters by the look of them, dressed in identical grey woollen suits and sturdy shoes. They sat beside Mrs Prosser and chattered both together, finishing each other's sentences, like ventriloquists. Next, a young couple—Mr and Mrs Williams, with his-'n-hers long hair, which made Mrs Prosser's nose twitch with disapproval.

Mom sent me to put the coffee pot on, and so I was

busy in the kitchen and didn't hear the creak of the front door opening. But I heard a man's voice, mumbling, and Mom saying, 'Please, come in, won't you?' Then the man's voice mumbled something else, and Mom said, 'Of course not. Please, come in.'

Suddenly everything around me went real quiet, like everything else had stopped. I started to run across the kitchen towards the front door, moving so slowly that it was kind of like a nightmare, you know? Like when a monster is after you and even though you're going flat out, you are moving about a yard an hour in your dream. The man at the door—Humphreys, the Troll's driver, out of uniform, a smile on his dark face—said something, I couldn't hear what. He shook his head, and then my Mom began, 'Oh, please, do . . .' And then I was heading for the front door like a rocket.

'Mom!' I bellowed at the top of my voice. 'The kitchen's on fire!' And I slammed the front door in Humphreys' face, knowing that whatever Mom did (and I knew I'd catch it, oh boy, would I catch it!) it would be worth it to stop her inviting him in for the third time and laying us open to . . . to . . . to what?

Mom squeaked and headed for the kitchen, and, real scared at what I'd done, (suppose he wasn't in league with Mrs Gwynne-Davies—suppose he was just an ordinary guy wanting to visit with us?) I waited for another, irate knock.

Mom reappeared, her face puzzled. 'Catrin Morgan, what's gotten into you? There is not either a fire in the kitchen! That poor man must think we're totally insane!'

I pasted on a sickly grin. 'Gee, I'm sorry, Mom. It was just a joke.'

'A joke!' Mom scowled. 'Not funny, Catrin. Where is he?'

'Who?' I hedged.

'Mr Humphreys. You know perfectly well who, Catrin. I'd just invited him inside when you pulled your stupid trick . . .'

'You know it, Catrin! Open that door at once! And wait until your father gets home!'

But when, hoping real hard, I opened the front door, there was no one there, and I heaved a sigh of relief. I'd avoided asking-someone-inside-three-times.

Throughout the evening I wondered who Humphreys really was: and every time Mom caught my eye she had a look on her face which meant Trouble.

And what an evening it was. I mean, I've sat through some real boring times, like Math lessons, but this was an all-time, world record, mega-hyper-super bore! Fat Mrs Prosser didn't contribute anything, although she ate and ate and ate until I thought she'd bust. And the others! Oh, boy.

The his-'n-hers guy ('call me Ifor') stalked about waving his hands in the air, reciting, beginning each line with these real weird noises. I couldn't decide whether the 'Oooooohs' and 'Aaaaahs' were part of the poems or not.

'Ooooooh! The soaring of the lark
Aaaah! The turtle awakes in the land
Snort! How blind are all our windows
Ooooh! Life has no meaning without you
Aaaah! You were my rainbow
Ooooh! And spiders are spinning me into their webs.
Snort! Do they understand?'

Well, I guess maybe the spiders might, but I certainly didn't, and from the expression on Mom's face she didn't, either. I caught her eye: she was purple with stuffed-up laughter. We all clapped politely at the end, except for the grey ladies, who muttered under their breath,

'Not portry, dear, is it? 'Tisn't portry if it doesn't rhyme!' which almost pitched me into giggles. Mom was trying to make believe she hadn't heard, but I knew she had.

Call-me-Ifor's wife didn't recite, she just gazed up at him adoringly while he paced and waved and Ooohed. Kind of nauseating, actually.

The grey ladies shared their poems between them the way they spoke, each saying a line in turn, and they were all sickly moony, spoony, Juney sort of poems that didn't have anything much to say, packed with little birdies and sunshine.

Man, that was one L-O-O-O-N-G evening.

When Mom had closed the door behind the last visitor—Mrs Prosser, of course, determined not to miss anything—she turned and glared at me.

'What were you thinking, Catrin, playing such a silly trick? Mr Humphreys must have thought you were mad, slamming the door that way! And the poor man was so shy he didn't even want to come inside the house. I'd just about enticed him inside when you played your idiotic game.' (*Yeah, Mom. So why didn't he stick around to be let in, later? And why did he need to be invited in three times, answer me that. Never mind, Cat. Don't explain, just apologise.*)

'Sorry, Mom. It was real stupid. I guess it seemed kind of funny at the time.'

'Well it wasn't. Pull a stunt like that again and you'll be grounded until you're too old to care, Catrin, understand?'

'Yes, Mom. Sorry, Mom.'

'OK. So we'll forget it. Just this once.' Mom's face

twitched. 'Oh, my goodness, Catrin, wasn't that the awfullest evening you ever spent in your whole entire life?'

'Mom. If you offered me the choice of sitting through another evening like that or poking myself in the eye with a sharp stick, I guess I'd have to choose the stick.'

'Oooooh!' Mom said, 'Why is the sky so purple?'

'Aaaah!' I said, 'Why do cows have knees? Snort.'

Mom clasped her hands in front of her chest. 'Tra-la-la,' she burbled. 'Pick a flower on the hour before a shower . . .'

'Can you see the green, green tree . . .' I began.

'Filled with birdies just like me!' Mom finished, and we collapsed in a heap, howling with laughter. I kind of thought the poetry Enthusiasm wouldn't last too long.

I told Twm about Mr Humphreys when we met on the bridge next day.

'So he is a Spoiler, too,' he said. 'Someone else for us to watch out for. You did well, Catrin. Did your mother punish you for slamming the door in his face?'

I shook my head, and giggled. 'No. The poems those guys read out were so awful she let me off. She was laughing too hard to get real mad.' Twm grinned. It seemed a long time since I'd sat wetly in a rock pool arguing with him. It felt like we'd been friends forever.

'What're we gonna do today, Twm?'

'I have to fetch some stuff from the shop for Taid first, but we could swim, after, if you want. You could show me how to ride that surfboard thing you've got.'

I looked at him sideways. 'A guy who swims with seals and talks to dolphins really needs surfing lessons. Yeah, sure, Twm: like a fish needs a bicycle.'

We strolled into the village, and I hung about outside the grocery store while Twm got Taid's shopping. The brass bell jangled wildly as he came out, and we were

113

heading towards Taid's cottage when Mrs Prosser, lurking by the Post Office, leapt out at us.

'Oh, sheesh, Twm!' I groaned under my breath, and Twm looked for someplace to hide. But there was nowhere. She'd gotten us, but good.

'I was jest wonderin', look,' she said, her chins wobbling, 'where did your Mam get that little table in the corner by the front door? Paid a lot for it, I expect, did she?'

'I really don't have any idea, Mrs Prosser,' I muttered, trying to edge past her.

'Of course, there's some might take exception to foreigners coming over here and buying up all our antiques just because they're rich, but I'm not like that.'

'No, Mrs Prosser.' Twm was edging away, trying to get to Taid's house and disappear.

'There's those,' Mrs Prosser went on, not even bothering to check if Twm was out of earshot, 'what might say, "now what's a girl like her doin' runnin' wild with that boy, even if she is a Yank?" There are, you know, I've 'eard em saying. "What does her Mam thinks she's doin'?" they're sayin'.'

I started to get my mad up. 'Twm's my friend, Mrs Prosser.'

As if she didn't care that Twm might hear, she bent towards me and said, 'He's peculiar, that boy. Not quite right, you know? Not sixteen ounces.' She tapped her head with her fat finger. 'You mark me, he'll come to a bad end. Just like his Mam.'

I knew my face was scarlet with fury. 'Goodbye, Mrs Prosser.' And I marched away from her, glad that Twm had managed to sneak out of earshot. I hoped he hadn't heard the horrible things she'd said about him.

I caught up with him at Taid's front door. He looked guiltily at me. 'Sorry, Catrin. I can't stand that woman.'

'Me either,' I said, all choked up with fury. 'She's horrible. She's an evil old dragon and she said you . . .' I stopped. 'Um,' I floundered.

Twm sighed. 'She said something about my mother, I expect?'

Mom says I'll never win prizes for tact, but I would rather untangle any knots in my friendships than wait for them to get so big they, like, strangle it, you know. 'What happened to your Mom, Twm?' I asked.

There was a silence long enough to make me wonder if Twm was ever going to speak again. 'Oh, frankfurters. Fat ones. Forget I asked. I was just—'

Twm kicked a stone along the path. 'I wish she'd mind her own business. I wish they'd all leave us alone.'

I followed him through the half-door into Taid's cottage and out back to where the old man was pottering in the yard, knee-deep in vegetables. Wigwams of bean-vines and sweet-peas poked up, and cabbages and peas mingled with raspberry canes. Butterflies were everywhere.

Taid looked up at the clatter of the back door latch, then straightened up at the sight of Twm's moody face.

'What is with you, Twm? You're looking like a wet weekend, *bachgen*!'

Twm, his hands thrust deep in the pockets of his shorts, looked at his feet. 'Mrs Prosser, Taid. Going on about Mam.'

The old man's face darkened. 'Trouble with that woman is she was born with a nose twice the length of everyone else's, and loves to stick it into other people's business.' He caught sight of me, standing behind Twm.

'Hello, now, Catrin. Come inside, the two of you. Let's

115

have a cup of tea, yes?' Inside the thick stone walls the air was cool, despite the heat from outside. A kettle hissed on the hob of the black range. Taid washed earth from his hands at the old stone sink by the back door and poured boiling water into the teapot. A black cat lay curled on a cushion, almost invisible in the shadows until it opened its green eyes to look at me, and yawned, showing a cavernous, red mouth.

'My Mam's cat,' Twm said. 'Tomos.' He still looked cross and out of sorts.

'There shouldn't be secrets between friends,' Taid said. I sat beside him on the stool, he looked at Twm as if to ask permission. Twm nodded.

'Good boy. Twm's mother was special, Catrin. When Twm's father died, Twm's mother went back to her people. She trusted me with Twm and Cei. But some people think that for a woman to abandon her children is the worst crime of all. But if the children know that they are loved, and that the mother does not want to leave them, but must, then they will understand, and forgive.'

'Back to her people?' I asked, puzzled. 'Was she foreign?'

Taid laughed, a peculiar, wheezy chuckle. 'In a manner of speaking, Catrin. In a manner of speaking.'

And neither of them said another word! I wanted to ask 'What people? Where? Will she come back? Why did she have to go? Why didn't she take Twm and Cei?' but I'd probably long-nosed it too much already.

We stayed and ate crusty bread and crumbly white cheese for lunch, and then spent the afternoon at the beach around the point beyond the Toll House, in and out of the sea with the surfboard. I was real mad that Twm was so good at catching waves—he seemed to sense exactly the right time to launch himself, and even managed to stand up once or twice.

Madoc ran along the tideline, investigating weed, barking at crabs and getting thoroughly sandy. Twm and I, exhausted, were lying side by side, our backs against the upturned dinghy, trickling sand between our fingers, when sudddenly the pup rushed back from the water's edge and began to bark. I sat up, and peered back along the beach towards the house, shading my eyes, trying to see what was upsetting him. I couldn't see anything: the house was hidden behind the rocky outcrop, but the dog yapped and yapped.

'Be quiet, *ci drwg*, you *twp* dog!' I said, showing off. But Madoc ignored me in both languages, making little rushes towards the house, and then back to where we sat, over and over.

'Hey, I think he wants us to go with him, Twm,' I said at last, not having watched all those *Lassie* movies for nothing. As if he had understood my words, Madoc stopped yapping and put his head on my knee, gazing at me steadily with his pale eyes. Twm sat up, slowly, and looked at him.

'I think you're right, Catrin. He is trying to tell us something.' We gathered up our belonging and set off home, following the excited puppy.

The Toll House looked OK. No flames licking at the drapes, no hordes of Red Indians besieging the ranch, no nothing. Maybe Madoc was mistaken. Maybe he just wanted his dinner. We let ourselves in through the back door to the kitchen, where Mom was sitting, at the table, writing, surrounded by what looked like half-an-endangered-rainforest's-worth of scrunched-up paper.

'Hi, Mom!' I said. 'Everything OK?'

117

She looked at me vaguely, as if she didn't quite recognise me, her eye-glasses on the end of her nose. She looked like a bemused owl. 'What? Oh, hi, honey, hi, Twm.' She looked at her wristwatch. 'Mercy! Is that the time?' She began collecting her paper and pens.

'What're you doing, Mom?' I asked, idly peering at the paper on the table. She snatched it from under my nose, turning pink.

'I'm writing poetry.'

I grinned at Twm. So the Enthusiasm was still going, despite the dreadful poetry evening.

'If they're coming again next week, Mom, I'm gonna be O-U-T!' I declared.

'No way, Miss Smartyboots!' Mom shook her head. 'One evening like that was one too many. But you recall slamming the door in Mr Humphreys' face? Well he came back today to apologise for not sticking around the other night, and guess what? He looked at some of my poems and said they were real good, and I should keep right on writing. And honey, ever since he came I've just been sitting here writing and writing, like he inspired me, y'know?'

I sat down, slowly, feeling dread creeping up my legs. 'How long did he stay, Mom?'

She looked puzzled. 'D'you know, honey, that's so odd! I can recall inviting him inside—' (at least three times, my mind said) '—and he was real shy, didn't want to impose, he said, in that funny way he has, but finally he came in and looked at my work. But y'know, I just can't remember him leaving! Isn't that wild?' Twm and I looked at each other, horror-stricken.

'Where is the Egg, Catrin?' Twm asked, urgently, and I flew out of my chair and up the stairs, flung myself between the curtains of the bed, and looked up at the canopy. The outline of the box was still there. I collapsed with relief. To make sure, I got the chair and climbed up. I opened the box, to reassure myself that the precious Egg was safe. It was.

Despite managing to get inside the Toll House, despite tricking Mom and bewitching her so that he could search my room in peace, he hadn't found the Egg.

CHAPTER TWELVE

Even though the egg was safe, I felt kinda nauseous—relief, I guess. 'It's there, Twm,' I said, downstairs again.

'What is?' Mom said. 'That old painted egg? Well of course it is, honey! Who'd want an old thing like that? It's precious to you, I know, but come on, you guys! That nice Mr Humphreys wouldn't take it!'

Oh yes he would! But I knew I'd never convince Mom.

Dad was home in time to eat with us, but for some reason he was real quiet. Maybe he was tired. The factory was opening in only a few weeks, and he was working real hard—but I got this weird feeling there was something else. I *know* my Dad, OK? Jake rattled on about fishing, and Cei, and this little black bug he'd found, and I think Mom was writing poems in her head and was miles away, and neither of them noticed Dad's behaviour. But I knew he had something on his mind. His hair was standing on end, too, where he'd raked his fingers through. He was real edgy about something.

We were into ice-cream and raspberries when he dropped his bomb-shell.

'The factory'll open right on schedule, honey. Isn't that great?' he said, heartily. Too heartily. Now, Mom noticed, and she kind of narrowed her eyes at him.

'Sure, David,' she said. 'Now tell us the bad news.'

'Gee, Kate. You are so suspicious!' Dad chuckled, which made Mom all the more suspicious.

Mom gave him her Hard Stare. 'There's something you aren't telling me, David. Something that will make me a real unhappy puppy? Huh, David? Speak, Oh-husband-of-my-heart!'

He grinned, sheepishly. 'Mr Takahashi's coming over for the opening,' he said.

'And?' Mom challenged. 'What else?'

'And-he-wants-to-stay-with-us. Not in an hotel,' Dad said quickly. 'Could you pass the butter, please, Cat?'

I passed the dish. Mom's face was a treat.

'He wants to stay *here*?' she said, weakly. 'You mean, like here, in this house? With us?'

Dad nodded, buttering his biscuit and reaching for the cheese. 'We have room, honey. And Mrs Takahashi just hates hotels.'

'*Mrs Takahashi*?' Mom whimpered. 'He's bringing his wife, also?'

It was a very l-o-o-o-n-g evening. Mom was—as they say over here—totally gob-smacked (great word, yeah?), and when she stopped being that, she panicked. Dad had to stop her rushing upstairs to scrub the guest room. I thought it might be kind of nice to have Mr Takahashi staying. I wanted to thank him for sending us here. OK, so I blamed him right off, and wished him hell-and-pitchforks, but now I was here—well, I felt kind of different, y'know?

Next day Twm 'phoned just after lunch to ask me to meet him at Taid's cottage. I was in such a rush to get out of the Toll House before Mom found me some chores to do that I ran down the road, and arrived bright red and out of breath.

I knocked on the door and heard Taid's voice calling '*Dewch i mewn*, Catrin', so I lifted the latch and went in. They looked kinda serious.

'This looks kind of like a council of war!' I said, nervously. 'Who's got um peace-pipe?'

Taid chuckled, his face wrinkled and brown as a walnut. 'Not a council of war, cariad. More a council of what on earth is happening! Twm told me about Humphreys. The Spoilers seem so anxious that I think we need to find the other Signs quickly. Twm. What do you think?'

Twm nodded. He had a real weird expression on his face—kind of happy and worried, all at once, as if he wanted something, but wasn't sure if he was allowed to want it. I guess that doesn't make sense, but *I* know what I mean, OK?

Taid went to a cupboard and brought back a bowl—an ordinary glass fruit bowl. Next he fetched a brown earthenware pitcher of water, a screw-top jar of what looked like dried leaves, and a box of matches.

Taid shook some of the leaves into the bowl and set fire to them. Clouds of sweet-smelling smoke rose up to fill the tiny room and made the black cat on the hearthrug sneeze. When the flames died away, Taid poured a drop of water into the bowl and mixed it with the ashes that were left behind, making a black paste which he smeared round the rim of the bowl with his thumb before pouring more water in to fill the bowl right up to the line of ash-paste, The still surface of the water shone in the darkening room.

The day was cloudy, so not a whole lot of light penetrated the small windows set low in the thick walls. But the room around us seemed full of shadows, because the only light came from the bowl itself, glowing an eerie blue-green. Taid stirred the water with his fingers and shook drops over all three of us, then, when the water in the bowl stilled again, he peered into it for long, long moments. At last, he sat back, shaking his head.

'Nothing,' he said, sadly.

'Let me try, Taid,' Twm said eagerly. But the old man shook his head.

'No, Twm. Wait until you are older.'

Twm scowled. 'I can water-scry as well as you, Taid. Mam taught me before she—before she left. She said if I ever really needed her she would come to me through the water.'

I listened, spellbound. If Twm needed his Mom? Of course he needed her! All kids need their Moms.

Taid sighed, deeply. 'I didn't know, *bachgen*. I am sorry. I am getting old and stupid, I think. Try, then, Twm.'

Twm slid the bowl towards him, and bent over it. The greenish light played on his face, making him look odd— kind of older. He frowned, concentrating real hard, and then, after a while, the frown cleared and was replaced by a huge grin. 'She's here, Taid! Mam is here!'

Beside the low-burning fire, the cat sat suddenly upright, expectantly. I peered hopefully over Twm's arm. All I could see was that real weird glow. And then, suddenly, that *wasn't* all I could see. A face was looking back at me! She had long dark hair and pale eyes like Twm's.

Twm spoke—in Welsh, darn it—so that I understood only around one word in twenty. The face smiled, and the lips moved although I couldn't hear her voice. Then she was gone, and Twm sat back, a thoughtful expression on his face.

'Twm?' Taid said.

'The man Humphreys *is* a Spoiler, of course, and the Gwynne-Davies woman, too. As we thought, Taid. They have seen the same Signs that I have. My mother does not know what the danger will be, yet—but she says that it will come from the sea with the next Great Tide.'

'What about the Egg, Twm?' I asked.

Twm nodded. 'It is the Sky-Egg, Catrin. The first Sign.'

'What about the Sea-Harp and the Earthstone?' Taid asked. 'Did she tell you where to find them?'

'No. She said only that they would come. When we have all three of the Sea-King's Signs we must go into the mountains to seek . . .' He stopped, suddenly, and glanced at me.

'What?' I said, suspiciously.'

The old man leaned back in his chair, his eyes meeting mine, as if challenging me to disbelieve. 'To seek Merlin's great mirror, Catrin. The Necromancer's Oracle. That will tell us all we need to know.'

The name buzzed round my head like an irritable bumblebee. 'M-merlin's mirror?' I said at last. 'You mean, like the Merlin's mirror in the legends? Like, you mean *that* Merlin?'

Twm nodded.

'Isn't Merlin just an old legend, Twm?'

'Like the Sea-Girl and the Sky-Egg, you mean?' Twm said, calmly. Something danced far back in his eyes that looked suspiciously like laughter.

I then had a Most Majorly Weird Feeling. The American half of me wanted to hoot with laughter, scream with panic, or rush out the door and all the way back to Pittsburgh shouting 'help, someone rescue me. They're all crazy as bed-bugs over here!' But the Welsh half of me just kind of blinked and said, 'Oh, yeah, right. Sure. Merlin's mirror. Yeah. Lead me to it,' and accepted it. Weird, or what?

I swallowed. Hard. Even I was surprised by what came out of my mouth! 'Right.' I said. 'So all we gotta do is wait for the other Signs, yeah? They'll be along soon, I guess. No sweat. *Dim problem.*'

Twm stared at me for a long moment, and then shouted

with laughter. 'She's one of us, Taid!' he chuckled. 'Welsh as the hills!' The old man nodded, smiling.

Inside, I glowed.

'By the way,' Twm said. 'My Mam sent you a message, Catrin.'

I stared at him. 'Your Mam? Me?'

'Mmhm. She sent you this—' and he put his arms round me, hugged me, and kissed my cheek '—and said I was to welcome the Sea-Girl home. *Croeso, Ferch-y-Môr*.'

I turned bright pink. You know, that awful hot feeling that starts at your toes and whizzles upwards? The words sure came from Twm's Mom, but I guess I knew the hug came from him!

'Sheesh, Twm!' I changed the subject, quick. 'What happened to Merlin, Taid? How come he lost his mirror?' (Which of course he must have, since Twm and me were going to go find it, later.)

Taid shook his head, sadly. 'Poor Merlin. Never could resist a pretty face. He fell in love with the wood-nymph, Nimue, who bewitched him. She led him a merry dance, and then shut him up in an oak-tree, forever, to keep him out of mischief. Some say he foretold his own fate—was plagued by great drifts of oak-leaves for the last few months of his life around the High King's court—found them everywhere, according to the legends. In his bed, in his meat, even blowing across the Great Mirror Itself. But that may just be a pretty story.'

'Merlin's Oak!' I said, remembering the story Dad had told me. 'Not the one in Carmarthen town?'

Taid chuckled. 'No, Catrin. There isn't enough left of that particular Oak to hide a beetle, let alone Merlin!'

I wondered how many oak trees there were in

Carmarthenshire and Ceredigion . . . And then, of course, there was Gwynedd, and Powys, and . . .

'So,' Taid said, 'now we wait for the other two Signs'. He got up slowly and poured the water from the bowl down the great stone sink in the corner.

The cat wound itself around my legs like a furry sigh, and I bent and picked it up, its lithe body warm in my arms, and wondered how long we'd have to wait.

CHAPTER THIRTEEN

When I got home, Mom was in the little study-room off the kitchen. I stuck my head around the door. She had a pad of paper in front of her, and was miles away, which was great, because I didn't feel like talking. I blu-takked a note to the fridge, and headed for the shore with Madoc for company.

I wandered along, picking up shells and tossing pebbles into the sea. Madoc nosed under clumps of seaweed—he has this real nasty habit of crunching up crabs, so their wiggly legs dangle out the side of his mouth. Yuk.

The sea was patched green and turquoise with a pearly sea-mist blurring where sea met sky. I conjured up a vision of dolphins leaping out of crystal water into the milky air, and sighed. I hoped Twm would take me there again, soon. In the States, sick kids swim with dolphins, and now I knew why. They were kind of peaceful.

The sun was slipping downwards when I turned to go back. The Toll House was a black shape in the distance, and by the time I reached it the lights were lit and Mom, poetry put away, was bustling about the kitchen making dinner.

It was Jake's turn to set the table, but I felt kind of mellow so I did it for him. He'd been to the library with Mom, and had his head buried in a book of old Welsh legends. I meant to read it, too, when he'd finished. *If* he didn't decide to begin at the beginning again immediately and start over! He does that, sometimes. I asked him why, once, and he thought about it for a while and then told me it was to see if the stories turned out different, second time around. I kind of know what he means! Mom's always real pleased when Jake reads anything. She worries he plays too many video games.

Dinner was real great: Dad had gotten home in time to eat with us, Mom had made my all-time favourite dinner, spare ribs and rice, and best of all everyone was content with their different days. Dad was in a real great mood, laughing, joking. He even mimicked the Troll, eating, peering suspiciously at his plate, and poking it with his fork, then shovelling it in as fast as he could.

After, Mom and Dad drank coffee and watched the local news on TV. There was a special business bit towards the end, then the newscaster made us all sit up, except Dad, who knew already what was coming.

> 'The new factory under construction near Cardigan for Takahashi, the giant American conglomerate, will come on-line at the beginning of next month.' [the announcer said] 'It was confirmed today that the President of the U.S. based parent company Takahashi (AmeriCorp), Mr Ito Y. Takahashi, will be present at the opening ceremony next month. The factory, which is built on a greenfield site near Pontpentre-dŵr, Ceredigion, will produce both components and finished assemblies for the domestic electronic appliance market.'

'TV sets and microwaves,' Dad said, as if we didn't know. The newscaster was still talking:

> 'The factory's Managing Director, an American proud of his Welsh ancestry, is Mr David Rhys-Morgan, who spoke to BBC Wales this afternoon.'

And there on the screen was my Dad, sitting in his brand new office!

'Dad!' Jake howled. 'You got to be on TV and you didn't say ONE WORD!'

Mom shushed him. 'Quiet, Jake. Let's hear what the good-looking guy on the tube has to say!' Jake pulled a barfing face, but did as he was bid.

Dad looked real good. He even looked kind of handsome, too! For an old guy, I mean!

'It's an honour and a privilege to be here in Wales on behalf of Takahashi Electronics. I'm real proud to be here, and Mr Takahashi will be flying in to Wales next weekend so that he will be here in good time for the official opening.'

When the newscast was over, Dad looked real smug. Mom reached over and ruffled his hair. 'Wow! Fame at last, and not before time! Do we need to pay to talk to you now?'

Dad polished his nails on his Pittsburgh Steelers Sweatshirt.

'No, I guess not. But a bit of respect now and then would be good, you guys!'

Then Mom realised what had been said on the telecast. 'Next weekend? You said *next weekend,* David! But the opening isn't for two weeks!' Dad nodded.

Mom gulped. 'Oh, David. That means I've got less than a week to fix up the guestroom. And I've just gotten started on my poetry.'

'I'm sorry, honey,' Dad said. 'How about I get you a tape recorder so you can talk your poems into it while you get the room ready?'

Mom scowled. 'No way would that work, you barbarian! I guess I'll just have to abandon writing until Mr and Mrs Takahashi have gone.' She collected the coffee cups and took them into the kitchen.

Her voice drifted back. 'That means I've got house guests for two weeks! Omigosh. I guess I'll just have to make the best of it.'

Dad winked at me. 'Will she survive without her Enthusiasm, Catrin?'

I put on a solemn face. 'I guess so. But, Dad, it will have to go someplace. The question is, where?'

We soon found out. Mom went into whirlwind mode. She cleaned the guest room until everything shone, and baked up a storm.

I escaped at the weekend, and met up with Twm. Early Saturday morning we took the boat out to the Island, away from the holiday crowds. Twm cut the outboard motor of the boat just off the island, threw out a line and in a very short time had caught two fat mackerel. The seals were less wary of me this time, and swam close to the boat, so I could stroke their sleek, cold heads.

We landed on the Island, and Twm built a fire in the hollow where the old house was, and roasted the fish on sticks. After, we rinsed our greasy hands in the cool springwater and set out to walk the island. Rabbits grazed unconcernedly, their white bobtails tucked away, seabirds wheeled over our heads and Twm pointed out things that I would have missed: butterflies and moths, small furry creatures; birds sitting on eggs, and on the far side of the island, where rough seas had worn away the cliffs into jagged teeth and it was impossible for humans to reach from either sea or land, the nursery coves where seals birthed their pups, nursing them until fluffy white changed to sleek grey.

As we walked back to the boat, the sun was beginning to sink in the west like a giant red balloon, leaving a scarlet trail along the glassy swell of the sea. The skin of my forearms prickled where the sun had caught me.

'I don't ever want to leave, Twm!' I said, happily.

'What, Wales? Or the island?' he asked, laughing.

'Both. Neither. I'd like to live on the island *forever*.'

'You'd change your tune pretty fast in winter, Catrin,' he said. 'I was here in November one year, with Taid. Cold enough to freeze us solid, it was, and the wind cuts like a knife. If Taid hadn't been with me I'd have frozen to death, I expect, but he showed me how to keep warm.'

'Why'd you do that?' I asked. 'Stay over in winter, I mean.'

'So Taid would know that I could, if I have to.'

'Why should you have to?'

Twm stopped, and looked hard at me. 'I'm different, Catrin. Haven't you noticed?'

I considered. 'You sure are.' I remembered that immature nerd Kurt Bonadetti and shuddered. 'You're kind of grown up, somehow, even though you're my age. And you know scads of stuff about birds and seals and dolphins, and you don't have a Mom or a Dad.' I stopped. 'No, you do have a Mom, but she's . . .'

Twm grinned. 'She talks to me from the bottom of a bowl of water.'

And yet it all just seemed kind of natural, somehow. I liked Twm, despite our bad start on the beach, and the little bit of magic I'd seen wasn't scary—the Sea-Egg, Taid and the face in the bowl of water. No big bangs, no monsters. I shrugged. I guess Wales was getting to me. 'I don't think you're so different, Twm.'

He shouted with laughter, scaring a puffin off the cliff.

'Duw, there's more Welsh blood than American in you, that's for sure. But I *am* different. I'm part *Tylwyth Teg*, Catrin. My father was human, but my mother was descended from Merlin, through Taid's line. We two are Sea-People, and our responsibility is to the sea-creatures.'

'I don't have fairies up *my* family tree!' I said, doubtfully. 'My Mom's New York Irish and my Dad's Pittsburgh Welsh . . .'

'And both Celtic. Don't they sometimes know things before they happen? Sometimes surprise you with things they couldn't possibly know?'

I nodded, with feeling. 'Sure. They always know when I'm in trouble. But I thought that was just Moms and Dads, not special.'

'Oh, it's special, Catrin. Your Dad's blood never stopped calling him home, even though he'd been born and brought up in a new country. It brought him here, and it brought you here, too, for a purpose. And when you got here, your Welsh blood told you that you were home, didn't it?'

'Yeah. It sure did,' I said, slowly. 'But it kind of scares me, Twm. This being the Sea-Girl and all. I don't know if I can handle it. Whatever "it" is,' I finished. I looked out to sea. On the horizon, tinted by the dying sun, sharp dorsal fins on graceful, curved backs slipped through the waves.

'I don't know, either, Catrin,' Twm said. 'But we have one Sign. We shall soon have the others, and then—we shall know.'

CHAPTER FOURTEEN

On the day the Takahashis were due to arrive in Wales, Dad went to meet them. They were helicoptering in to the factory landing pad, which Jake thought was majorly impressive—I guess maybe he was hoping for a ride . . .

Meantime, Mom roasted a leg of Welsh lamb, and fretted, because nobody had thought to ask if Mrs. Takahashi was vegetarian! But she wasn't, and when she groaned 'Man, oh man, I'd kill for a coffee!' as she kicked off her neat high-heeled shoes in the living room, Mom knew that everything was going to be just fine.

Mrs. Takahashi was so tiny. Her wrist bones were smaller than Jake's, and her skin was wonderfully creamy against her blackbird hair. She'd been born in Japan but had lived most of her life in New York, so she and Mom had loads in common. Before she'd been in the Toll House an hour, they were chatting away like long-time-no-see-um-buddies.

Eventually, Mr. Takahashi said 'Tell me, Catrin. Have you forgiven me yet for sending you to the, ah, the "back end of nowhere", wasn't it?'

I blushed, and glared at Dad for telling. 'I guess so, Mr. Takahashi. I hated it, first off, but now I love it.'

Mr. Takahashi nodded wisely. 'I thought that you would. I thought so.'

Over lamb roasted with garlic and rosemary, dinner turned into quite a party. The Takahashis treated me and Jake like grown-ups, so Jake told Mr. Takahashi all about his book of Welsh legends, which started Mr. T. in on dragons, and how they turn up in so many cultures the world over, so he believed they had probably been real, once. Then Dad started in on Mom's Enthusiasms.

'My wife,' he said, when we were all sitting round after dinner, 'my wife, having stripped every antique from every shop in west Wales, has now turned her Enthusiasm to poetry.'

Mrs Takahashi groaned. 'Oh, Lord, David. Don't start Ito talking about poetry! He writes Haiku, and will lock himself away for days at a time to get them absolutely right!'

'Haiku?' Mom asked, pricking up her ears 'What's a Haiku?'

Mr Takahashi delightedly explained, while Mrs. T. covered her eyes with her hands and pretended to cry.

'Haiku is a Japanese poetry form that consists of seventeen syllables—usually arranged in one line of five, one of seven, then five again. It is very, very small poem,' he added. 'Very, very difficult to get right.'

Mom's eyes glazed over, and I knew that her Enthusiasm had taken a turn for the worse. 'Show me!' she demanded. I could almost hear her counting syllables in her head.

'We shall write Haiku together, I promise,' Mr. Takahashi said, his eyes twinkling. Mrs. T. raised her eyes to the ceiling.

'I can see I shall have to amuse myself,' she said, resignedly.

'I'll help,' I promised. I liked Mrs Takahashi. 'I mean, I'm here. I guess I could keep you company—if you don't mind. If you want me to,' I floundered, not sure if I was being kind of pushy. I just remembered she was my Dad's boss's wife!

'Would you show me the seashore?' she asked. 'I just

love the ocean. And there is an island! Could we rent a boat, maybe, and go see it?'

'I could ask my friend Twm,' I said, doubtfully. 'He's got a boat. He might take you out.' But I wondered if Twm would welcome a stranger to his island. He might get mad at me all over again for suggesting it.

On Monday we all had to get dressed up and go see the new factory. We toured the big, low building, full of people sitting at benches putting electronic bits and bobs together, and then ate lunch in the staff canteen with the workers, and then Mr. Takahashi and Dad and the Chairman of the County Council held a press conference. Mom said all this show-biz stuff would go to Dad's head. Before we left, Dad introduced us to his new Secretary, Mrs Williams. She was busy organising the celebrations for the official opening. Dad called her his 'Welsh Dragon', but she was real nice and friendly. I could tell Mom liked her, too.

Just after tea (traditional American this time—fudge brownies and pecan pie) Twm bashed on the dragon's-head knocker. I invited him in, but he shook his head.

'We need to talk,' he whispered, urgently. 'Meet me on the bridge tomorrow morning. I'll be there at eight.'

'Sure!' I said. I closed the door behind him, and wondered if he'd found another of the Signs.

I sneaked out of the house real early—before anyone else was up. It was a cool, damp morning, with rain-clouds banked over the sea, so I wore a sweater over my T-shirt. Twm was there before me, and his expression didn't cheer me up any.

'Taid looked into the bowl again last night, Catrin. He says we need to find the other Signs, before it is too late. Only days we have left before the danger comes.'

I didn't like the sound of this. 'Does he know what, yet? Did the bowl tell him?'

Twm shook his head. 'Only that it will come from the sea.'

I thought of sea-monsters and drowned cities, and shuddered. 'Where do we look?' I asked, helplessly. 'The Signs could be anywhere.'

'Taid said we must begin with the Island. I told him we've walked it end to end, but he is certain the second Sign is there somewhere. We must go early tomorrow. Six o'clock, so that we catch the tide.'

I thought about that prospect. Dawn, as far as I was concerned, was for the birds. 'The Takahashis don't leave until Sunday, but I should be able to get away one day, at least.' I checked my watch. 'I've gotta get back—family breakfast for the Takahashis' benefit today. By the way, Twm—Mrs. Takahashi would like to see the island before she leaves. Could you take her out in the boat? She's real nice, and we don't need to land if you don't want.'

Twm frowned. 'I don't like taking strangers out. Once people are seen landing, all the tourists will want to go. Tourists will wreck it.'

I sighed. 'OK I'll tell her no. I guess she'll understand, she's a nice lady.'

Twm scuffed his sneaker in the dust of the bridge. 'Oh, all right, Catrin. But I won't call the dolphins.'

'That's OK,' I said, happily. 'She'll get to see the seals, and I know she'll just love that. Thanks, Twm.'

Twm laughed. 'She'll see the seals. They're more curious than she is. We'll take her out this afternoon if you like.'

Mrs. Takahashi was delighted.

'But we can't land on the island,' I warned. 'Landing would disturb the wild-life.'

I saw Mom open and shut her mouth as if she had been about to say 'Oh, but you and Twm land'. But she obviously thought better of it, praise be!

'But that's just wonderful!' Mrs Takahashi said. 'Just going out in the boat will be great. Gee, I sure miss the ocean, living in the city. When I was a kid in Japan, I lived right close to the seashore, and spent half my life in and out of salt water.'

The dampness of the morning burned off, the sun came out, the clouds disappeared and the afternoon was hot and windless, with a sea like cobalt glass. Mrs. Takahashi and I wore shorts over our swimsuits, and Twm just shorts. He greeted Mrs. T. politely (I was kind of scared he might be sullen, because he didn't want to take her, but he was OK). Especially when he realised she knew her way around boats—she was in, and sitting down, as soon as we were afloat.

Mrs Takahashi turned her face to the sun like a flower, trailing her fingers in the sparkling water. Nearing the island, she saw the nesting colonies of birds. She told us how Japanese fishermen used cormorants to catch fish by putting rings round their throats so that they couldn't swallow what they caught, which seemed kind of cruel to me. Then she spotted the orange, white and black clown-faces of the puffins peering warily at us from their ledges, so that when the first seal arrived she didn't notice, and they had surrounded the boat before she spotted them.

When she saw the sleek, dark heads, she made no sound, just smiled and stretched out a hand. Twm grinned, obviously expecting the creatures to disappear, but instead they came close, jostling the little boat to be in reach of her hands, like puppies, begging for her attention.

'They like you!' Twm said, astonished. 'They trust you!'

Mrs Takahashi looked up, pushing a wing of midnight hair back from her face. 'Of course,' she said. 'I am a sea-person too. I was born beside the Great Sea and under the Sign of the Fish. They know me.' Mrs. Takahashi made a huge hit with Twm.

CHAPTER FIFTEEN

I set my alarm clock for 5.45 a.m.—and pulled the pillows over my head and groaned pitifully when it went off. The birds were shrieking the dawn chorus as I slipped out the back door, and the sun made a diamond of every dew drop meshed in a spiderweb. Twm was waiting, the boat already launched, and the sea was covered in pearly mist which beaded in our hair and eyelashes. The early morning was chill, but once the sea-mist burned off it would be real hot again. I had to be back home by mid-day, because Mom wanted me to go with her and Mrs Takahashi to see some castles and stuff. But because we'd gotten up so darn early, we still had a real long morning to hunt for the other Signs. Twm nosed the boat into the jetty and we scrambled ashore.

Then, beginning with the beach itself, we searched the Island end to end, looking for anything that might be a Sign. The Sky Egg had found me, although I hadn't known it, but the Sea-Harp and the Earthstone were keeping themselves real well hidden! We searched the cottage from top to bottom, climbed most every tree, combed the grass around the spring, peered into a hollow oak, poked down rabbit holes, tiptoed round roosting birds and ducked angry flying ones, turned over every rock and rummaged in every cave. And found nothing. Zilch. Nada. Zero.

Twm flopped down on the grass, his elbows resting on his knees, his chin on his forearms. 'Taid was so sure the other Signs were here. Or one of them, at least. But there's *nothing*. Can't you feel *anything*, Catrin?' he pleaded.

'No, Twm. I wish I did. I'm sorry. I'm such a wipeout.

A major failure. Maybe there's been a mistake and I'm not the Sea-Girl.'

'You are!' Twm said, fiercely. 'My Mother said you are, and so you must be.' He rose and offered his hand to pull me up. 'Come on, let's have a swim before we go back. Taid will be disappointed, but we did our best.'

He allowed the little boat to drift into deep water, and then dropped the anchor-stone. Shucking off his shorts, he arrowed off the boat in a perfect shearwater dive, scarcely making a ripple. I followed soon after, and the coolness after our long, hot, frustrating morning was wonderful.

And then the dolphins were with us. 'You *are* the Sea-Girl,' Twm said, shaking wet hair out of his shining eyes. 'The Sea-People wouldn't allow you near if you weren't. Come on, Catrin. Dive with me.'

The sea-bed was far below. 'Let yourself go, Catrin,' Twm said. 'Keep your eyes open and just—sink. Don't worry. You won't drown, I promise.'

So I took a deep breath, trusted, stopped treading water and let the waves close over my head. Sinking, I opened my eyes. The sun dappled the surface of the sea above me, and our slipping shadows patterned the sandy bottom. A shape glided up to me, and a dolphin gazed earnestly into my face, its fins wafting gently.

I reached out a hand, slowly, slowly, and stroked the smooth skin, and I could feel the water cold on my teeth. I was smiling. I seemed to have been underwater for ages, but felt no need to go to the surface to breathe.

'Come, Catrin,' Twm said, taking my hands in his. He spoke some few words in Welsh, and we sank together, hands linked, smiling into each others' faces until I felt the sandy bottom silky beneath my feet. Looking up, the dark outline of the boat bobbed on the surface, and about our heads the dolphins flew like waterbirds, and sleek seals twisted and curved around us.

I was calm, relaxed—and breathing, under water!

A dolphin whistled in my ear—and I understood! 'Welcome home, Sea-Girl,' it said. I pinched myself. I had to be dreaming! Twm was beside me, the sunlight marbling his laughing face. 'Sea-Girl!' he said. 'Sea-Girl, Sea-Girl!'

I captured a passing fin and clung on tightly as the dolphin twisted and curved, our linked bodies occasionally breaking the surface as we danced. I'm a good swimmer, but this was not swimming. It was flying, effortless, free, streaking through my own element.

The dolphin took me further and further out to sea, but I wasn't afraid. And then it dived, pulling me down to the sea-bed far below. This was deeper than I'd ever been: Mom would have had a triple-dip conniption with extra nuts if she'd seen me! Her constant shriek on the beach was 'Don't go out of your depth, Catrin!' She'd purely die if she saw me now!

On the sandy seafloor, in the weed-covered ribs of a sunken boat, something gleamed. The dolphin paused above it, and flexed, shaking me free, and I knew it was telling me to swim down to it.

I stroked down, effortlessly, my hair streaming back from my face like weed, and I picked up the shining thing. It was a shell, large, the outside creamy white, a smooth, translucent pink at its core. Stretched across the open mouth of the shell, fastened with tiny silver bars through holes bored in the outer rim, were row upon row of harp strings. I stroked my fingers across them, and crystalline music rippled in my mind, although I knew that I could not possibly hear it, underwater. I had found the Sea-Harp.

The dolphin nudged me, and again I clasped the strong

141

dorsal fin, the Sea-Harp clutched to my chest as we flowed like the wind in a cornfield back to shallow waters and Twm. My companion touched noses with me, and then, as silently as they had come, the dolphins were gone. Surfacing beside the boat I placed the Sea-Harp safely inside, and pulled myself after it. Twm was soon beside me, grinning like a Cheshire cat.

'Taid was right!' he crowed. 'The Sign *was* here! Only one more now, Catrin, and we have all three.' He hauled up the anchor stone, started the outboard motor and we chugged slowly into shore. I carefully wrapped the Sea-Harp in my T-shirt and put it safely in my ruck-sack. Then I lay back against the side of the boat and trailed my hand in the water, remembering the cold, silky feel of it all round me, and the cool resilience of the dolphin's skin. On shore, the trees hiding the Toll House were a dark green mass in the distance. Suddenly something hidden in the trees flashed, catching the sun.

'Twm,' I said, realising what it was. 'I think somebody's watching us. In the trees. Don't turn round. They've got binoculars or something.'

Twm's triumphant grin disappeared. 'The Spoilers will try twice as hard, now, to get the Signs. You'd better come back with me and talk to Taid.'

On the village road, I kept looking over my shoulder in case we were being followed, even though it was bright daylight, and I held very tightly to the Sea-Harp.

In the cottage, Taid's hands, holding the Harp, trembled. 'The second Sign,' he breathed. 'At last.'

'Catrin saw someone watching us from the woods, Taid,' Twm said. 'The Spoilers saw us.'

'I doubt they'll risk trying to break into the Toll House,' Taid said, thoughtfully. 'Not yet, anyway. They'll probably wait until Catrin has all three Signs and then try to get them. When you have the Earthstone—that is when you must be careful, Sea-Girl.' His blue eyes shone in the dark cottage. 'I think you know, now, that you are the Sea-Girl, Catrin, yes?'

I nodded, completely certain, now. 'Yes. But Taid, what if the Spoilers steal the Harp and the Egg and then go find the Earthstone themselves? What's stopping them doing that?'

Taid thought about it. 'It's possible. Look here.' He took a small paper packet from a shelf in the dresser. 'Take this. It is all I can do to protect you, if they come. If any of them should try, sprinkle the powder over yourself, and on the Signs if you can. But I don't think you need to worry, Catrin.'

Oh boy! How wrong can one nice, kind old guy be!

CHAPTER SIXTEEN

That afternoon Mom, Mrs Takahashi and me tromped round just about every castle in west Wales, and Mrs T. shot about a zillion rolls of film. Now usually I just love looking at real old places—American history is kind of— well—short, unless you count the Native Americans, but they didn't build any castles! But that afternoon half of me was climbing dizzy-making spiral staircases, and the other half was at the Toll House with the Sea-Harp and the Sky-Egg.

I'd thought about hiding the Harp with the Egg, on top of the bed canopy, but decided I needed to find someplace else, because if the Spoilers did come looking, I didn't want to make it easy for them. In the end I went into Mom and Dad's room and hid the shell harp inside her purple velvet squishy hat, inside a hatbox on the top shelf of her closet. This hat she wears in the depths of winter when no one is likely to see her. She says it makes her look like a goblin under a toadstool!

But bits of me twitched all the same. That evening, I had a real worrisome thought. What if the 'inviting-three-times' thing gave the Spoilers kind of a free pass into the house? What if Humphreys could get in any time he liked? I fetched Sea-Harp and Sky-Egg, both. The safest place for them was in bed with me, so no one could steal them while I slept, not without waking me. I tucked the Egg under my pillow, where I could feel it, sticking lumpily into my ear, and after a bit of thought I put the Shell into my Garfield p.j. case and cuddled it.

Madoc's barking woke me, long before dawn, because the room was real dark. The window is too low down and the walls too thick for moonlight to get in, and at first I lay drowsily wondering why Madoc was fussing. I sat up, and thought about getting out of bed, but then heard Dad downstairs, hushing the puppy.

'Hey, you crazy hound!' he said. 'Hush up! We're trying to sleep. What did you hear? An owl? A cat?' I heard the back door open. 'Take a look, you hairy dum-dum. There's nothing out there.'

I woke right up. Maybe nothing was out there then, but *something* had disturbed Madoc, who, OK, was kind of hairy, but no dum-dum. What had been outside? And worse, was it now in?

I put on my light, and shoved Garfield and the Egg right down my bed, under the covers. The packet Taid had given me was beside my bed, and I opened one end of it, just in case. It was full of brownish/silvery powder, like sand and crushed seashells, and smelled seaweedy and kinda peppery. I sat up in bed, straining my ears, but heard only Dad going grumpily back to bed. The packet poised, I got up and gingerly opened my closet door. Sheesh, I hated doing that. I guess I've seen too many movies where horrible things fall out of closets! But it was empty, except for my clothes.

Then, out of the corner of my eye I saw the curtains stir, although the window was shut. Maybe a draught from closing the closet? But the rosy pattern on the curtain was kind of blurred, like—how can I describe it?—like the way a heat-haze shimmers above a freeway on a real hot day. Something was in the room. Mrs Gwynne-Davies, when she had set fire to the hearthrug, had moved so fast only I could see her. A figure moving incredibly fast might look kind of blurry, like that . . .

For a minute I froze, then, stretching nonchalantly,

yawning, the open packet concealed in my right hand, I pretended I was gonna get back in bed. I faked another yawn, covering my mouth with my other hand, and kinda stumbled closer to the blurry air beside the window. I could feel a sort of wind on my face, the closer I got, and then, fast as I could I sprinkled the powder all over the blur and all over me, and then rushed to the bed, pulled back the bedclothes, and sprinkled the Harp and the Egg, too. Then I did a *real brave* thing. I gathered the Egg and the Harp to my chest, scrambled into bed, and pulled the duvet right up over my head!

Why Mom, Dad and Jake didn't come running, as well as the police from the next three counties, I'll never understand. The noise was so incredible I had to look! Remember that old movie, *The Wizard of Oz*? Where the tornado hits the house? Well, that's what my bedroom was like. Vast winds screamed and howled round it, whirling my robe up into the air and my gorilla slippers and the bedside rug, my books on my bookshelf, and a magazine from the dressing table. The duvet, too, lifted slightly, but I grabbed it and pulled it over me like a turtle-shell, and crouched over the Egg and the Harp. Round about then, I stopped looking. After what seemed like hours, when it had gotten quiet again, I got brave enough to stick my nose out from under.

The room looked perfectly normal. Everything was in its place. My gorilla slippers were neatly side-by-side next to my robe, the books were back on the shelf, everything as it had been before the tornado hit. Amazing.

I sat up, kind of stiffly, and looked around me. No shimmery bits of air, so it looked like Taid's stuff worked. I still had the Signs and the Spoilers had gone. But it was a long, long time before I slept again, and when I did, I slept with the light on.

Twm was real worried next day, and we hurried to Taid's to tell him, too. The old man shook his head. 'They know you have the two Signs, so you must take them with you everywhere, Catrin. Because your mother invited the Gwynne-Davies woman's driver inside, the Spoilers can get in when they want. The Signs are not safe in the Toll House.'

Oh, great, I thought. I get to carry the Signs around with me so they can ambush me in broad daylight! Oh, wow! Major mega-fun!

Taid gave me more little packs of powder, and something else. In the corner of the room a curtain concealed a flight of stairs, and Taid creaked up these, returning with a piece of red cloth. Inside, on a chain, was a tarnished silver locket covered in a twisting, knotted design. Taid slid his thumbnail into the crack, clicking the locket open. There were no tiny photographs inside, only a strange black curl of something brittle. It didn't look so hygienic, to be honest.

'What is it?' I asked. If it wasn't real important I'd empty it in the nearest trashcan.

'Seaweed,' Taid said. 'All that the Prince of Cantre'r Gwaelod had left of his Sea-Girl. The Prince kept it until he died. And here it is. Protection, Catrin.' Twm fastened the locket round my neck, and it hung down inside the neck of my T-shirt.

'Um,' I said 'Would it be OK if I kind of polished it up some? No one would wear anything this tarnished from choice, Taid. If I use Mom's silver polish, it won't look so strange to other folks.'

Taid laughed. 'Of course, Catrin. It is yours, now. Polish it until it shines like the moon, if you wish.'

Twm interrupted. 'According to the legend, Taid, the third Sign was hidden at the source of a river. But which river? And will the Earthstone still be there?'

Taid leaned back in his chair. 'The river that flows through the village to the sea beyond the Toll House. And it will still be there, if no one has taken it,' he said.

'That's like saying tomorrow will be fine unless it rains,' Twm muttered.

'It is, indeed,' Taid said. 'But Catrin's the Sea-Girl, and she has two Signs, so it is likely that she will find the third.'

I had to check with Mom that it was OK for me to spend the whole of the next day with Twm. Mrs Takahashi dropped real big hints that she'd enjoy a ramble up a river bank, but luckily Mr T. had other plans, which got me unhooked.

Before I tucked me, the Egg and the Harp up in bed I got Mom's silver polish out of the cupboard and shined up the locket. Once the ugly black tarnish had gone, it was real pretty. I opened it up and touched the dried seaweed. It fizzed like sherbet on my fingertip, and I jumped, and shut it again, quick.

That night I dreamed of a girl with pale skin and dark red hair, swimming in and out of the ribs of a sunken galleon . . .

Mom packed up lunch for Twm and me, and I tucked it in my rucksack with the Signs. When we got back, maybe I'd have the third Sign. I wore the locket, which Mom (of course!) spotted straight off.

'My, honey, that's so pretty!' she said admiringly. 'It looks real old, too. Where did you get it?'

'Taid gave it to me,' I said, through honey and wholemeal toast. 'It *is* real old, I guess.'

'But honey, how odd that he should give it to you! I'd want to give such a lovely old thing to my daughter, or my grand-daughter. It's an heirloom.'

'Well, Twm's Mom doesn't live with them, and Twm's a guy,' I said, not really wanting to get into a discussion about either the locket or Twm's Mom!

'Well,' Mom said, still not satisfied. 'I guess one day Twm will marry, and surely it should go to his bride?'

I shrugged. 'Maybe, Mom. But Taid gave it to me. Hey, what if I give it to Twm before we go back to the States?'

Mom is real romantic about generations, stuff like that. When she married Dad she wore her Great-Grandmother's wedding gown and veil, and she's got it safe in storage back in Pittsburgh so that I can wear it when I get married. Like, yeah, Mom! Not only am I not getting married, ever, but since I am already a half-inch taller than Mom right now, by the time I am old enough to get married (which I will not!) the darn thing won't fit me anyway. Mom is kind of small, and Jake and me take after Dad, size-wise.

Right then Mr and Mrs Takahashi came down to breakfast, and I took the opportunity to escape.

I met Twm on the river bridge, and we began the slow trek towards the source of a river, bubbling out of the ground.

CHAPTER SEVENTEEN

Actually, we cheated some. I was expecting to walk the whole distance, but we rode the bus part way. The only bus I ever rode in Pittsburgh was the school bus from home to school and back each day. This was real different: the driver was, like, a delivery guy as well! We stopped by outlying farms to deliver parcels and newspapers, so we went all over, kind of sight-seeing. I'd have enjoyed it, but even though I had the Sea-Girl's locket and Taid's powder, I still felt kind of scared. We thought we knew, more or less, where the Earthstone was, but so did the Spoilers, also. And what if they followed us and stole the Signs from me?

When we left the bus, no one got off with us, and no one seemed to be lurking nearby. We waited until the bus disappeared, then climbed over a wooden stile, following a footpath across a field to the river.

The summer had been real dry, so the river wasn't high, but it was clear and cold, running noisily over small boulders and pebbles. We waded upstream awhile to cool off after the bus-ride, but the water was so icy our feet went numb, so we quit and walked the bank instead.

Twm showed me turquoise kingfishers like flying jewels, and watervoles, pied wagtails bobbing like wind-up toys, and brown trout lurking in the trailing waterweed. The river began to narrow, and around noon, we stopped for lunch, on a sunlit bank, trees dappling overhead.

Walking again, after we'd eaten, the path became narrower and narrower, and steeper, and got kind of rocky. The river shrank to little more than a small, tumbling stream. We followed it upward until, just below the top of the hill, with what seemed like the whole of Wales spread out below, we found its source bubbling out of the ground from beneath a big, sheltering slab of stone like a propped-open lid.

We put down our rucksacks so we could look beneath the rock slab. I guess I expected the Earthstone to be sitting inside, maybe flashing like a bubble light on a police car, just like that. But there was only water, bubbling over rocks. Twm sat back on his heels, frowning.

'It must be here somewhere!' he said, running his hand through his hair, so it stuck up in damp spikes.

I felt around with my hand in the icy water, and pushed down against the fiercely bubbling flow in the hope of feeling anything like a box. Nothing. I felt like kicking something real hard. I slumped back on the ground, leaning against Twm's rucksack. We hadn't found the Earthstone. My hand slipped to the Sea-Girl's locket around my neck. I fingered it, feeling like I'd failed her. I guess maybe I touched the catch, because the bit of dried seaweed fluttered into my lap. I grabbed for it, but the wind took it, blew it into the spring, and the bubbling water carried it downstream.

My eyes followed it. It seemed to be getting bigger. And greener! I scrambled after it, *knowing*, somehow that the Sea-Girl was helping us. 'Bring the rucksacks, Twm!' I hollered over my shoulder, and puzzled, he followed me.

The scrap of dark green weed caught on a rock downstream. I looked around and under the rock, expecting to find the box with the Earthstone. I was so certain! But I was disappointed again. Brown gravel stirred, mud eddied, and a small fish shot for cover, but that was all. I patted the streambed with my hands: nothing. I took off my sneakers and waded into the shallow water, first upstream, then downstream, from the weed, feeling with the sensitive soles of my feet, real careful. Nothing.

I gave up. I turned and took a step towards Twm.

'Ow!' I hopped, grabbing my toe. 'Ow. Shoot! That hurt!' I was so busy examining the blood dripping from my hacked toe that it was *Twm* who found the box! Or what remained of it.

I'd bashed my toe on a pair of crossed iron bands so flaked and rusted that the metal was holed like lace. Inside the iron, half-buried in the gravel stream-bed, slimy with age and long immersion—was a stone. Oval, smooth, with a hole in the middle. In the hole was a second, rougher stone, shimmering with embedded crystals, so tightly wedged that I could only turn it inside the other stone, not remove it.

'The Earthstone,' Twm said. 'Catrin—you have the third Sign.' His grin stretched from ear to ear. He gave it to me.

I felt the Earthshock as soon as I touched it, tingling up my arm like electricity. This Sign was different from the other two—it felt dangerous.

We grinned at each other like lunatics, did a bit of dancing and yelling, then calmed down some and sat beside the stream with the Earthstone on the grass between us, and celebrated with the last can of cola.

Packing up, I said, 'What'm I gonna do with the Earthstone, Twm? I can't take it into the Toll House, can I? We won't have a house any more if I do!'

Twm considered. 'Taid'll know.'

I tied the rusty iron bands around the Earthstone with my belt, so my nylon rucksack wouldn't biodegrade into crude oil, instantly!

Walking back, we laughed a lot, and ran crazily downhill, and at first neither of us felt the strange, cold wind. Twm noticed it first, when we were almost back to the stile, and stopped so suddenly I cannoned into him.

'Ow!' I complained, as my nose hit his rucksack. 'What d'you stop for?'

'Shh!' Twm grabbed my wrist, pulling me back into the wood. 'Look!'

A strange column of dead leaves, like a six-feet-tall whirlwind, was moving along the riverbank. Above it, green leaves were changing colour, drying out—and falling, in the middle of summer! A second column of spinning air, close to the riverbank, whipped the grass into flat brown circles.

'Spoilers!' I hissed, wishing I was someplace else. 'Twm, they've got us!'

'No, they haven't,' he whispered, grimly. 'Where's Taid's powder?' I fished in my rucksack, found a packet, sprinkled a little over the Signs, and shook the rest over Twm and me. I rummaged inside the rucksack for a second packet, and when I looked up, Twm had disappeared.

'Twm?' I whispered. 'Where'd you go? Don't leave me!'

His voice was so close to my ear that I jumped. 'Here.'

'Where?'

'Right beside you. Look harder.'

I did look harder, but still I couldn't see him—and then I could. He wasn't invisible, exactly. He just kind of blended in like a chameleon.

'Wow!' I muttered crossly. 'Real neat, Twm. But what about me? They can still see me. *I'm* still here.'

'No you aren't.'

'I am so!'

'Oh, for goodness sake, look at yourself, Catrin!'

He was right. I wasn't there, exactly the same way he wasn't.

'What do we do now?'

'We keep very quiet, Catrin,' he whispered patiently, 'very, very quiet.'

I held my breath, and we shrank back into the trees, both of us watching the approaching spirals of air. Cold wind blew my hair about, and dead leaves whispered and rustled about my ankles.

The whirlwinds slowed and stopped, leaves drifting to the ground. Two figures appeared: Humphreys and Mrs Gwynne-Davies, large as life and twice as ugly, standing between us and the stile to the main road.

'Where are they, Humphreys?' the old lady asked crossly.

'Search me, Madam,' Humphreys said. 'They was here just a second ago.'

'I know that, you idiot!' Mrs Gwynne-Davies snapped. 'But where did they go?'

'Search me, Ma'dam' Humphreys repeated. 'They was—'

'I know, I know. Here just a second ago. Don't just stand there, you buffoon. Find them! That girl's ginger hair stands out like a beacon—surely even you can spot that!'

I'd opened my mouth to say 'I do not have ginger hair!' when Twm's almost-invisible hand clamped over my mouth.

'Mmmph!' I said, crossly.

The old lady spun round like a witch in a storybook! I kind of hoped she didn't have a gingerbread cottage hidden away in the wood someplace . . . But she couldn't see us.

Humphreys poked half-heartedly in a bramble bush, getting real scratched up in the process, and Mrs Gwynne-Davies prodded him from behind with her walking-cane, nagging at him like toothache. After a while, he straightened up, removed her stick from his ribs and said

154

'They isn't here, Madam. They've give us the slip, somehow, looks like.'

Mrs Gwynne Davies lowered the stick and raised her head, sniffing the air like a dog. 'But they are here, Humphreys! *I can smell them.*'

'Fee,fi,fo,fum,' I thought, stifling a giggle. Twm caught my hand, and removed the second packet of Taid's powder from between my fingers. Stealthily he crept up behind the Spoilers and sprinkled the powder over them. What on earth was he doing? We surely didn't want them invisible, too! I needn't have worried.

'Ahem,' Humphreys said, scratching his leg. The old lady scratched the back of her neck. Humphreys scratched his arm. She scratched her side. Humphreys took off his chauffeur's cap and scrabbled at his head. The old lady raked her chin.

'Drat!' Mrs Gwynne-Davies said crossly. 'I appear to have been bitten.'

'I, also, Madam,' Humphreys said, pulling up his trouser leg and scratching a skinny white shin on which a pattern of large red blotches was appearing.

The rash was springing out on Mrs Gwynne-Davies's face as if someone was sploshing her with a paint brush, and I clamped my hands over my mouth so that I wouldn't laugh. I'd have guessed poison ivy, except it doesn't grow in Wales.

The Spoilers lost interest in us, and hobbled off, scratching furiously, down the path to the stile. We watched them get in their car, and still scratching, drive off, before we ventured out. I kind of hoped Humphreys didn't meet any other cars, because he was swerving all over, trying to scratch and drive at the same time.

'How do we flag down a bus if we're invisible, Twm?' I

asked, and then realised that away from the trees, we weren't. Taid's powder,' I said thoughtfully. 'How d'you reckon it works? It made a whirlwind in my bedroom, made us invisible, and now Humphreys and the Old Troll are itching like crazy! But all the powders look the same.'

'Think,' Twm said. 'When you woke up and discovered the Spoiler in your bedroom, what did you do?'

'I sprinkled it with powder, jumped into bed, pulled the duvet over my head and—' I stopped. 'Y'know Twm, the weirdest picture popped into my head. Did you ever see *The Wizard of Oz*?'

Twm laughed. 'Only every Christmas since the year dot.'

'Well, I suddenly thought of when the tornado strikes, and Dorothy's house is blowing away, and the old witch rides past the window on her bicycle . . .'

'—and then you had a tornado in your bedroom,' Twm finished.

'And when I sprinkled us, I thought *quick, hide*,' I said, thoughtfully.

'And when I sprinkled them,' Twm said 'I thought *distract them, somehow*. Taid's powder seems to do more or less what we need it to.'

At the bus stop we checked the schedule. There was one due any minute.

'So you'd better be very careful what you're thinking when you sprinkle that stuff about!' Twm said.

I had to agree.

CHAPTER EIGHTEEN

We went, right off, to tell Taid. I was so excited and all, I had one foot over the doorstep before I remembered the Earthstone! I put on my brakes, fast.

'I can't!' I said. 'The house will fall apart!' Twm went in, to consult with Taid.

'It's all right,' he said. 'The Earthstone only works when it's touching something man-made. If you carry it, it's safe. Just—don't put it down anywhere, please!'

'I guess I get to sleep standing up, the rest of my life!' I muttered, going inside.

'No, Catrin,' Taid said. 'Don't worry. Twm, boy, go into my shed. On the shelf above that pile of seed-trays, there's an old box. Fetch it in by here, please.'

Twm did as he was bid, bringing back a small iron box.

'Now give me the Earthstone,' Taid said, and I undid the buckles of my rucksack, untied the iron bands and handed the Earthstone over. Without thinking, Taid put it on the stone-paved floor while he opened the catches on the box.

The square, flat stone kind of fizzed, and vanished, leaving an earthy hole in the kitchen floor. Twm scooped up the stone, fast, and popped it into the open box. Taid fastened the catches, and laid the box—real careful this time!—on the floor, then we all kind of held our breath and waited for the roof to fall in. It didn't.

'What now, Taid?' I asked. 'We've gotten all the Signs.'

Out came the brown bowl, in went the burning leaves, then the water from the earthenware jug, and there was Twm's Mom again. This time I could see her a whole lot clearer.

Which was just as well, because it was me she wanted.

'Catrin?' I heard her voice inside my head, soft and deep, like a middle size church bell.

'Yes, Ma'am?' I answered.

'Sea-Girl!' she laughed. 'Do not be so formal. I am . . .'

'We've gotten all three Signs, Ma'am,' I said, quickly. I wasn't quite ready to be on first-name terms with a—a—a whatever she was. 'What next?'

'You must find the Necromancer's Mirror. Twm?'

'Yes, Mam?'

'Go where the sea reflects the mountains. Find the Oak.'

Twm nodded.

'You and Catrin must go alone. Father, you may not help. You can only advise.'

Taid sighed. 'I know it, daughter.'

'First, find the Mirror. Then, you will know.'

I was getting a cricked back from sitting up straight. Twm's Mom kind of held the attention, you know? If she'd been a teacher, she sure could have taught me math!

'And then, Sea-Girl, you must use the Signs.'

'Yes, Ma'am,' I said, nodding. 'Um. Will it be dangerous?'

The face in the water smiled. 'Almost certainly,' she replied. 'But you have the Signs, and the Sea-Girl is immortal.'

I kind of doubted that—but then I remembered swimming with the dolphins, the tornado in my bedroom, and realised that since I didn't know doodly-squat about magic, who was I to argue?

'When must we go?' Twm asked, and the Lady's eyes closed, as if she was looking deep down inside herself. At last, she said, 'Tomorrow. Before the next great moon. You have no time to waste. You must go tomorrow.'

The image faded, and the room seemed darker without the glow from the bowl.

'Tomorrow,' Twm said.

'Tomorrow,' Taid agreed.

'Tomorr—oh, shoot!' I said. 'Tomorrow Mom is taking me and Jake and Mrs Takahashi to this hippie-type place in Mac- Machyn - '

'Machynlleth,' Twm finished. 'The Centre for Alternative Technology. It isn't a hippie-type place.'

'Whatever. I can't get out of it, Twm! Can we hold off on Merlin's Mirror—say until Friday?'

'My mother said no, Catrin,' Twm replied, firmly.

I chewed my lip. Planet-saving comes before polite, I guess. 'Right,' I said. 'Mom will ground me until I put down roots and grow apples, but I'll sneak out real early and come over.'

'She'll understand,' Twm said.

'She won't,' I replied. 'Trust me. When Mom makes a plan, NOTHING stands in its way.'

I spent kind of an uncomfortable night, partly because my brain was telling me that Mom was gonna go ballistic, and partly because sharing a bed with a large, spiky shell, a lumpy egg and an iron box was not a relaxing experience.

Next morning, my alarm woke me at sunrise, and I got up and dressed, putting the Signs into the rucksack. My shoes in my hand, I stopped by the kitchen and left a note:

> Dear Mom
> Sorry, can't go today. There's something I've got to do. I know you'll be real mad, but I'll explain later. Don't worry.
>
> Hugs and kisses, Cat.

I hadn't intended to take Madoc, but he flung himself at my ankles and opened his mouth to bark. I hurled myself at him and grabbed his muzzle. 'Shhh! Quiet, Madoc! OK, you can come too. But please, puppy, please, please, please, hush up!' He quivered for a while, snuffling against my hand, then relaxed. Slowly, I released his nose, ready to grab it if he opened his mouth again. We slipped out of the house and over the garden wall, because the gate squeaks. The Signs were knobbly in the rucksack on my back, and the dew soaked through my sneakers. Sleepy birds muttered in the trees, and mist rose from the river like smoke.

Taid and Twm were up already. I accepted the bread-and-honey sandwich Taid offered me, and Madoc came in for his share, too. 'I had to bring him,' I explained, 'else he'd have barked and woken Mom. Should I leave him here with you, Taid, or take him?'

Taid considered, rubbing Madoc's ears thoughtfully. He squirmed with delight, and licked Taid's hand.

'Given the way you are going to travel,' Taid said, 'Madoc had better stay with me. Cei can take him for a walk, later.'

'Do we hop a bus?' I asked. 'How far is it?'

'It's a long way. Too far for the bus,' Twm said, and grinned.

'Then how? We can't drive.'

Taid twinkled. 'There are other, quicker ways.'

I looked from one to the other. 'Like, how?'

I soon found out. Twm took hold of my hand, and Taid got out more of his silvery-brown powder.

'Remember what the powder does, Catrin?' Twm asked.

'It kind of does what we want,' I said, uncertainly. 'But—what do we want?'

160

'We want to go to North Wales, extremely fast,' Twm said. 'Keep that in mind, and don't leave go of my hand.'

I shut my eyes, tight, as Taid approached with the powder.

'Keep them open, Catrin,' Taid said softly. 'There's nothing to be afraid of.'

I don't know what I expected—kind of 'Beam me up, Scotty', like *Star Trek*, I guess. But it wasn't like that at all! I once saw a film of a jetplane, coast-to-coast, where everything kind of flickered past before you could focus on it. It was just like that. Castles, villages, towns, fields, rivers, hills, rushed past, and then, there we were, side by side, on a green clifftop. Before us the sea stretched, a green and blue patchwork, and a large island rose offshore. Behind us a range of vast blue mountains reached to a cloudless sky.

'Where are we?' I asked.

'Where the sea reflects the mountains. Your hair is standing on end,' Twm said.

'Yeah, so's yours. So *where*, Twm*?*'

'Once upon a time,' Twm said softly, 'here on this spot stood the summer palace of the High King. Beautiful, it was, and mighty. Out there is Ynys Môn, Anglesey, and behind us is Eryri. Snowdon. There are waterfalls, rivers, lakes. And a cavern. And the Mirror.'

Turning my back on the sea, I looked around me. 'That's a lot of mountain, Twm,' I said. 'Too big, I'd say, to kinda just stroll in, pick a cave and find the Mirror. Where in heck do we start?'

Twm took something out of his jeans pocket, and showed me on the flat of his hand. It was a small silver disc, with a hole bored near one edge where a chain or thong could be threaded. It was beautifully decorated on one side with a pattern of oak-leaves and acorns, and on the other a full grown oak tree.

'It belonged to an ancestress of mine. She once—um—knew Merlin quite well.'

Something in his manner made me suspicious. 'Would I have heard of her?' I asked.

'I think so. It was Nimue,' he said, and blushed.

'Nimue! That was the person who—'

'Shut Merlin up in an oak,' Twm mumbled.

'So how do we use this to find Merlin's cave?'

'The one person who knows not only where Merlin is, but where his Mirror is, is Nimue.'

'Was Nimue,' I corrected.

'*Is* Nimue.'

'Oh.'

'If I hold this, and concentrate hard, it should lead us to the cave.'

'On foot, or by beam-me-up-Scotty?'

'Taid's powder,' Twm sprinkled us both, and grabbed my hand. 'Now, concentrate, Catrin!' he ordered.

'What on?'

'Finding the cave, of course!'

I'd hardly gotten my brain booted up before we were whizzing cross-country again. Forget roller-coasters—even the new betcha-die-of-fright ones, this was worse, especially whizzing up and down the mountains. It was—aaargh! I'd have screamed if I'd had any breath.

Then we were standing in a small wooded valley half way up a mountain. A river ran through it, and rocks shouldered out of the ground, like the mountain was flexing its muscles. The whole place felt kind of 'keep off', y'know? Especially the dark cave-mouth up the hill a

162

ways. Twm got a torch out of his rucksack, and had started towards the cave.

'How do we know this is the right cave?' I asked, following reluctantly. Twm took me by the shoulders and turned me round. Behind me was the biggest oak tree I've ever seen. It was probably prehistoric.

'Merlin's oak,' Twm said.

I expected the cave to be dank and dark, but it was dry, and smelled of woodsmoke. It wasn't a large cave. 'Uh. How big is this Mirror, Twm?' I asked, doubtfully, looking around me.

'Very, I think,' Twm said. 'I've never seen it, of course, but it sounds like it's big, in the legends.'

'Then this has to be the wrong cave. There's noplace in here you could hide even a vanity-mirror.'

Twm sighed. 'This is the right cave. Use your eyes, Catrin.'

I looked, but I still couldn't see anything.

'Remember by river, when you couldn't see me?' Twm said. 'Try to look the way you did then.'

I kind of let my eyes go out of focus. At first nothing was different, except I felt real dumb—and then I noticed the door.

The huge, iron-bound-and-studded threatening-looking wooden door at the back of the cave.

It looked real scary.

'Oh, shoot,' I said.

CHAPTER NINETEEN

The door was locked, and I felt kind of relieved about that!

'Aw, too bad, Twm!' I said, insincerely. 'I don't see any key.'

Twm scowled. 'It has to be here somewhere, Catrin. Help me look. Where could it be?'

I looked around the cave. 'Mom hides the spare key to the Toll House in the outhouse under a flowerpot,' I said helpfully.

'No flowerpots!' Twm said. 'But plenty of rocks. Start turning, Catrin.'

I began to turn over stones, large and small. My legs started to ache after a little while, and I straightened up and cracked my head on an overhanging ledge. 'Ow!' I said, then had a thought, and fingertipped along the rocky sticking-out bit. I felt something cold, and key-shaped and brought it down. It lay across my palm, huge, black, and kind of sinister. 'Oh, Twm!' I said, smugly. He turned round.

'Where was it?' I showed him. 'Right. We must put it back before we leave.'

He put the key into the lock, but was bright red and puffing before the key finally creaked round and the lock clicked open. He pushed at the door, which opened with kind of an *Addams Family* creeeeaaaak. Oh, I really, really did not want to go inside! And then a glimmer of light caught my eye. Light? In a cave? I followed Twm inside, and gasped.

The roof arched like a rocky cathedral inside the mountain, and crystals in the bare rock gleamed and glinted in the light of dozens of flaming torches in metal brackets on the walls.

'Er,' I said, 'how come the torches, Twm?'

'I think we are expected, Catrin,' Twm whispered.

'Like, by who?' I stammered. 'Nobody knows we're here, Twm!'

'Except my mother,' Twm reminded me, 'Mam knows.' That made me feel kind of better—I guess.

Greenish brown straw-type stuff scuffled under our feet; rich red and green tapestries glowed like jewels on the walls, and a huge table, covered with a dark red cloth, occupied the centre of the cavern.

'Um, Twm?' I asked. 'Does anybody live here?'

'No. No one since Merlin.'

I nudged him. 'He left his robe behind. Look.'

A dark green gown smothered in gold-embroidery glinting in the flaring torchlight hung from a hook on the back wall of the cave, and a tall, pointed and rather battered star-strewn hat hung from a carved wooden chair beside a rough wooden bed. Sheepskins heaped the bed, tumbled, as if someone had just gotten out from under. If I touched the lumpy pillow, where the hollow of a head showed, might it still be warm? Twm's voice interrupted my thoughts.

'Help me with the cover, Catrin.'

We grasped a side each of the red cloth, and lifted it clear, folding it and laying it on the bed. I slid my hand across the pillow. I'm not sure if I was disappointed to find it cold, or not!

The Mirror lay on the table, its vast moon-shape reflecting the torchlight and the crystals studding the vaulted roof. It kind of reminded me of the *camera obscura* on Constitution Hill, in Aberystwyth. You could see all over, even Snowdonia on a clear day, the guy in charge said, only it was overcast the day I was there. But tiny, inch-high surfers caught waves off the beach, and matchbox buses slid through the town, and once, the guy said, they'd even seen someone cheating on a golf course miles away!

I peered into the Mirror, but all I saw was me. An oak leaf, brittle, brown, lay on the silvery surface, and I blew it off. Twm was reflected upside down across the table.

'What now, Twm?' I asked. 'I don't see anything.'

'The Signs, Catrin,' Twm suggested, and I opened my rucksack and took out, first the Sea Harp, its silvery strings glinting in the light. Next, the Sky Egg, and finally, the Earthstone. I placed them one by one, on their own reflections.

For a moment, nothing happened, and then, in the centre of the great mirror, something stirred, like wind-blown fog. The Sea Harp tingled out a rush of sound, and in the mirror I saw what *looked* like my reflection. Only I knew it wasn't. Couldn't be, because my reflection was right where it should be, under my nose. And yet there was another me in the middle of the mirror!

'The Sea-Girl!' Twm whispered.

Her hair was darker than mine, and her pale face was pointed as a cat's. Her eyes were strange, huge and fully green, without any sign of white. She wavered, and her hair drifted about her face. Smiling, she revealed small white teeth. 'You have my Signs!' she said, delightedly. 'Oh, please, give them back to me?'

'In time, *Tywysoges*,' Twm said firmly. 'First, please tell us what you know. When you have told us, and when we have used your Signs as they were meant to to be used, then you shall have them, I give you my word.'

'You swear, Necromancer?'

166

Pardon me? Then I realised that she hadn't looked at me at all. Did she know I was there?

'I swear, Sea-Girl,' Twm replied gravely, and reached out across the mirror to lay his hand flat on the surface. The girl raised her own hand, and, one hand up-side-down from beneath, one hand stretching out above, they touched palm to palm.

The Sea-Girl closed her eyes. It was real weird looking at her—kind of like looking at me, or at how my twin sister might have looked if I'd had one.

'Tell Gwyddno Garanhir,' she whispered, 'that the sea-walls of Cantre'r Gwaelod will be breached at the Equinox . . .'

'No, Sea-Girl,' Twm said, gently. 'That is past, Cantre'r Gwaelod is long gone.'

She sighed, sadly. 'Ah. Have I slept so long? I remember, now.' Her image in the mirror wavered, and angry seas swirled about her small, pointed face. It looked like a real bad storm—one that would go right off the storms-at-sea scale. Great dark waves rose, swelled, and crashed, and lightning flashed, illuminating a sky filled with looming, threatening black clouds.

'This is loads of help,' I muttered. 'A storm. Somewhere at sea. Big deal.'

'Shh!' Twm said, his eyes on the mirror. 'Look!'

A huge ship lurched wildly in the pounding, towering waves. Its long, flat deck, sluiced by torrents of water, would have washed the oil-skin clad sailors overboard if they had not been tethered to ropes stretching end to end on the deck. The name *Kyoto Star* was lettered on the bows.

Then, suddenly, another ship was tossing, close to the first—too close. A passenger ferry, huge bow doors concealing ranks of cars and lorries, lightless, rolled helplessly, as if it had no power or steering mechanism. Beside the first boat it looked like a bathtub toy.

I held my breath, wanting to shut my eyes, not see it. It was obvious what was going to happen. The bigger ship ploughed into the smaller one. I could almost hear the rending crash and the screams of the people on board the ferry, although the vision in the Mirror was silent. Both ships were holed, and the passenger ferry began to sink, so quickly that within minutes it was gone, leaving only a flurry of bubbles, bits of floating rubbish—and people, helplessly bobbing in the tumbling water.

Twm frowned. 'A collision? That can't be it!' he said. 'That's terrible, tragic—but it wouldn't harm the Sea-People! That can't be the warning, Sea-Girl!'

Horrified, I watched the mirror. 'Look, Twm,' I said. 'Look what's happening.'

A huge hole in the side of the bigger boat gushed torrents of black, thick, liquid, spreading ugly black fingers on the surface of the sea, rolling like black cream on the waves, stretching out towards a place I'd seen only in pure, bright sunlight. A tiny jetty, steep cliffs, puffins, guillemots, shearwaters, seals, dolphins, porpoises . . .' I shut my eyes. I didn't want to see any more.

'Oil,' Twm said, dully. 'The *Kyoto Star* is an oil-tanker.'

'The Island will die,' I said, my mind showing me pictures of seabirds thickly coated in oil, and seals swimming, blinded, through the dreadful, choking stuff. 'What's the point in showing us all this? We can't stop it if it has happened! Oh, Twm, everything will all die.'

Suddenly his shoulders straightened. 'No, Catrin! Don't you understand? The Sea-Girl is showing us what *will* happen, and where—*if we don't stop it*! We have her Signs! We can prevent it!'

'They won't believe us, Twm!' I reasoned. 'Who's gonna believe a couple of kids?'

Twm picked up the Sea-Harp, and rippled the strings. 'Oh yes they will, Catrin! We have the Signs!'

We turned back to the mirror. The pounding seas had gone, and the Sea-Girl was back. 'When, Sea-Girl?' Twm asked urgently. 'Tell us when.'

The Sea-Girl shimmered, sunlight dappling her underwater face. 'When the moon is full, Necromancer,' she said. 'When the sea rages and the wind is high. On such a night my Father took back Cantre'r Gwaelod. You have my Signs. Use them well—and when you have done, remember your promise. You gave your word, Necromancer!' And she was gone.

We covered the mirror, and I packed the Signs away in my rucksack, slinging it on my back, shrugging my arms through the straps. The dead oak-leaf shifted on the floor, and I picked it up, wanting to leave the cavern tidy, for Merlin's return. We locked the door of the cavern behind us, and put the key on its ledge. Outside, I laid the leaf under the giant oak tree, and put my hand flat on the rough bark. I took it away again, real quick, because the oak throbbed with power . . .

Twm sprinkled us with powder, we held hands and travelled—boy, did we travel—arriving almost before we left on the bridge near Taid's cottage. We ran down the road, eager to ask Taid what we should do next.

But a few yards from the front gate, I stopped, and grabbed Twm's arm. 'Twm, wait!' I whispered. 'There's something wrong . . .'

CHAPTER TWENTY

Twm stopped, puzzled. 'What?' he asked.

I pulled him back down the road and into the doorway of the village shop, out of sight of Taid's cottage.

'I don't know. I just have this real bad feeling.'

Twm looked at me, hard. 'Catrin, I'm listening! What's wrong? Concentrate.'

I concentrated. Something was kind of nagging at me. The bell on the shop door tinkled, and a man pushed past us, opening a pack of cigarettes, and across the street a woman tugged a small, wailing child along on a wrist strap, like a puppy on a lead . . .

'That's it! Twm—*Madoc isn't barking!* He would have heard me coming a mile off. He barks to wake the dead.' Then I had another thought. 'Unless, maybe—did Taid say Cei would take him out for a walk?'

'He did.' Twm looked at his watch. 'But it's twenty-past-two, Catrin, and Cei has football practice on Thursdays in the holidays between two and four. He never misses. So,' he said, frowning, 'what's going on? Come on.'

We left the village the way we'd come, climbed over a fence into the field behind the cottage, and crouched behind the tall hedge at the end of the garden while we decided what to do.

'You wait here,' Twm said, getting down on his hands and knees. He crawled through the hedge, trying to pick the place where it was thinnest, but got real scratched up anyhow—red streaks appeared on his bare arms. He slipped silently up to the kitchen window and peered cautiously inside. Then he crept around to the front, out of my view. Seconds later he was back, his face grim.

'The Spoilers are inside,' he whispered. 'With Taid.'

'Shoot, Twm, what're we gonna do now?' I asked. I didn't want to tangle with the Spoilers. I was tired. And scared.

'I still have one of Taid's powders, remember? Open the rucksack, Cat, so I can sprinkle the Signs. Then I'll do us.'

I busied myself with buckles. 'Yeah, Twm, but *what do we want the powder to do?*'

Twm considered. 'Getting inside the cottage without them seeing us would be a help.'

He sprinkled us, and I watched him blend into the hedge and disappear, even though I could still 'see' him.

We tiptoed forward, and then stopped. 'If we go in the door, Twm, they'll see it open and know we're there even if they can't see us.'

'I've thought of that,' he replied. 'My bedroom window's open. We can leave the Signs there, and creep downstairs and get behind them. Can you climb the apple tree OK?'

'Sure I can!' I followed him up into the swaying branches, hoping the sound of the rustling leaves and unripe apples bouncing off the grass wouldn't attract attention. Twm went headfirst through his window, and I followed after. His room was small, with low windows to the floor, a small bed with a patchwork spread, and shelf after shelf of books. In the brief time I was in there, I saw at least six I wanted to borrow—and that was before I reached the shelf of books on Welsh legends and magic . . .

'Come on, Catrin,' he hissed from the doorway, 'this is no time to be assessing my library.'

We crept down the narrow, crooked staircase. Halfway down he stopped. 'Be careful. The next step creaks,' he whispered, and we both did giant steps over it, holding on to the hand-rail so as not to stumble and make a noise.

Twm pulled the curtain back an inch or two, and peered round, then slid it silently back all the way. The Spoilers had their backs to us, but I recognised Humphreys' tall skinny shape, the back of his neck still blotched and looking real itchy. I didn't recognise the other person at first, and then I recognised the dreadful woman who had upset Twm by talking about his mother—Mrs Prosser, that was it! I wished I had a sharp pin to stick her with, since she couldn't see me anyhow!

Taid was facing us, sitting in his chair, but I couldn't see Madoc anyplace. I went cold. Suppose they'd hurt him—what if they'd killed him!

Taid shifted slightly, and looked straight at us: he knew we were there.

'When the girl and the boy comes back, if they hands over the Signs, we won't harm them,' Mrs Prosser said. 'We wants them Signs. They don't belong to you. And if you got any sense, you'll give 'em us.'

'You are right. They are not mine,' Taid retorted. 'But neither are they yours, woman. They belong to the Sea-Girl.'

'And you think that American kid is the Sea-Girl? Rubbish. Just a tourist, she is, like all the rest. Nuisance, that's what they are.'

That's all YOU know! I thought.

'Whether she is or she is not, she has the Signs. And she will keep them, I shall see to that,' Taid said.

'All them Yanks is soft in the head. Stupid, they are,' Humphreys chipped in. 'All we've got to do is knock you about a bit and she'll hand them over, no problem. We may not even have to hit you, much. Just threaten, like!' Trouble was, he was probably right. But he hadn't finished. 'Or we could do the dog. That'd do it for sure!'

Now I was getting my mad up. I was gonna go ballistic, any minute. And when I blew, they'd be real sorry! Twm put a hand on my arm and I managed to unclench my fists and stop grinding my teeth. He beckoned me back upstairs. Once inside his bedroom, he whispered 'I'm going down the tree, and I'll come in the front door. I'll make a noise, pretend I'm talking to you, so you'll know exactly when I'm coming in. Then, while I'm opening the door, you sprinkle them with the powder.'

'What do I wish for?' I asked. Then I remembered Humphreys' plans for Taid and Madoc. 'Never mind,' I said. 'I'll think of something.'

Twm climbed through the window and down the tree, and I crept silently down the stairs again. I heard Twm's voice coming up the garden path.

'Catrin,' he said, so loudly I thought sure they'd know he was pretending 'What a good day it's been, hasn't it?' he said unconvincingly.

Oh, great! I thought. *Now talk about the weather, why don't you?* He'd never make it as an actor, so I hoped he didn't plan to try! Then I heard him rattle the doorknob, and I flung back the curtain and sprinkled the Spoilers, fast, thinking real hard about what I wanted to happen to them.

Fat Mrs Prosser was sitting in a wooden chair with arms, and the arms grew hands and wrapped themselves around her, holding her tight. Humphreys didn't turn round, so he didn't see the huge brass vase float through the air. But he sure felt it when it went 'byoinnnnng' on the back of his head. His legs gave way, and he folded in a heap on Taid's flagstones.

'Beat up on Taid, would you?' I said. 'Kill Madoc, huh? Not while I'm around, you great turkey!'

Mrs Prosser, wrapped round in strong wooden arms, stared at the talking air with her mouth wide open. Twm's feet appeared, followed by the rest of him, and he swiftly tied up Humphreys, who was just coming round. I'd only given him a *light* tap, honest. Then he knelt beside the old man.

'Did they hurt you?' he asked, fiercely.

Taid shook his head. 'No. I was afraid you might not realise that they were here and come rushing in. It would have all been over if you had. They would have taken the Signs.'

'Catrin knew that something was wrong when Madoc didn't bark,' Twm explained.

'Where is he, Taid?' I asked, urgently. 'He's OK, isn't he?'

'He's in the wall-cupboard,' Taid said. I rushed across and peered inside. It was real dark, and right at the back, with his legs tied, was Madoc. I could see his shadowy head moving, and I reached in and lifted him out. He was whimpering softly.

'They put rubber bands on his nose, Twm!' I said. 'Man, oh man, now I'm *real* mad.' The puppy whined, and I gently removed the horrible things. They'd left a groove in his soft muzzle and I kissed it better. Madoc licked my nose, and when I'd untied his feet he leapt around me as if he was on springs, yapping hysterically.

'Madoc!' Twm said sharply, and the puppy stopped immediately, and sat to attention, his tongue lolling, but every nerve and muscle was straining, he wanted to jump around so much.

'They didn't harm him, Catrin,' Taid said. 'He was frightened, but he's all right.'

'They were gonna kill him, Taid!' I said fiercely. I

174

glared at Mrs Prosser. 'How'd you like it if I put rubber bands on *your* nose, huh?'

'Calm down, Catrin,' Twm said. 'We have to decide what to do with these people. We have more important things to do than worry about revenge, remember?'

'Oh, yeah?' I said, still cross. 'Oh. Yeah.' I remembered the Mirror, and the oil-tanker.

'Even with the Signs,' Mrs Prosser said smugly, 'you're not strong enough. And you still have to convince somebody that something will happen. And who's going to believe a ginger-headed Yankee brat and some *twp* Welsh boy? Everybody knows you aren't sixteen ounces, Twm ap Sion.'

'I am not either Yankee!' I yelled. 'I am at least half-Welsh, and my HAIR IS NOT GINGER!' Twm snorted. 'Oh,' I finished up, 'and Twm is not either *twp*. So now, you—you—you old bat, you!'

'So what do you think you're going to do with us?' Mrs Prosser asked, finding her tongue. 'You got to let us go. You can't do nothing else. Mrs Gwynne-Davies has got magic, she has. She'll sort you out, just you wait.'

'But her magic doesn't work when I'm around,' Taid said, mildly. 'Didn't you notice? Which is why she sent you and Humphreys. If she'd been able to use magic, she'd have come herself. She'd have enjoyed doing far worse to me than you ever could.'

Mrs Prosser's face fell. 'Oh,' she said, and was silent.

'So what *are* we going to do, Taid?' Twm asked. 'We have to work out who to warn, and when, and how—and we can't do that if we're worrying all the time about these two.'

I had a sudden thought, and beckoned Twm over so that I could whisper. 'Are there any other Spoilers?' I asked.

'Besides Mrs Gwynne-Davies, I mean. Because if there are others . . .'

'Yes.' Twm said. 'There are always four—but we don't know who the other one is, yet.'

Taid stood up, carefully, stiff and shaky from sitting in one position for a long time. He straightened his back, kind of creakily, and when he was upright, he smiled. He went to the cupboard, and brought out a small square metal cage. 'I think I know what to do with our friends here,' he said. The cat, which had been lying on the hearthrug, pricked her ears and sat up straight, watching his every move, as if he knew . . .

Taid put his hand on Humphreys' head. And Humphreys shrank! And shrank and shrank, and grew a long nose, and a longer tail. The cat crouched, lashing her tail, but Taid was too quick. He picked up the white rat and popped it in the cage. Mrs Prosser squeaked.

'Don't you DARE do that to me!' she said. 'Don't you d —squeeeeak!'

She made a wonderful rat. Even the cat didn't want to get too close.

CHAPTER TWENTY-ONE

Taid clicked the door of the cage shut, and put a padlock on for good measure. The rats sat miserably in the corner. I had a thought. 'Taid,' I said, slowly, 'why didn't you use your magic powder on them?'

Taid's face was worried. 'I didn't use it, Catrin,' he said 'because the first thing they did when they'd tied me up was find my powder and put it in the fire. It's all gone, I'm afraid.'

'Can't you get more?' I asked, alarmed.

Taid shook his head. 'The ingredients have to be collected from different places at different times. It depends on the moon, Catrin, and the pull of the tides. There is no time to make more.'

Twm opened his rucksack. 'I have two left, Taid. But only two.'

'Then you must be careful how you use them,' Taid replied. 'In the meantime, tell me what happened today.'

I glanced nervously at the cage. 'Won't they overhear?' I whispered.

'They will,' he replied. 'But what can they do about it?'

'I think Catrin's right,' Twm said. 'The Spoilers have Messengers, Taid, the way I have the dolphins, the seals, the birds . . .'

'They do?' I looked around, half expecting something with two heads and a whole lot of teeth to hurtle out of the closet.

Taid sighed. 'You're right, my boy. I am getting old, and addle-headed.'

'What sort of messengers?'

Twm shrugged. 'Spiders, cockroaches, wasps—who knows. Mrs Gwynne-Davies had a pet carrion crow, once.'

'What happened to it?'

Twm gave me a long, level stare. 'I think it drives her car.'

'Humphreys?'

'Humphreys appeared about the same time as the crow vanished. So who knows?'

The Humphreys rat was sitting up on its hind legs, beady red eyes watching us. Listening. We went into the garden, away from the rats, and hoped that none of the wasps and worms around us was anything but a wasp or a worm . . . Twm told his grandfather what the mirror had shown us, and in my mind I saw again the terrible, creeping tide of thick, black oil.

'Remember when that tanker grounded on St Anne's Head in 1996, Taid?'

Taid nodded. 'There were Spoilers at work there. A simple accident became a terrible disaster, because of the Spoilers.'

'All that coastline,' Twm went on, 'all those birds, thousands of them, oiled and dead. The birds—I was down there, then, helping wash them, remember? Puffins, guillemots, scoters. And the seals—so curious they came to look, didn't they, surfacing in oil slicks miles long, burning their eyes, poisoning them. They shovelled it off the sand, and tried to scrub it off the rocks, for the tourists, but it will be years before the sea-creatures recover. We can't let it happen again, Taid, not here. Not in Cardigan Bay. Not my Island. I won't let it. Taid, the name of the tanker is the *Kyoto Star*, and we know a car-ferry will be involved—but we don't know which line, or the name of the vessel. The Sea-King's Daughter said the accident will happen—what did she say, Catrin?'

'She said "When the moon is full, and when the sea rages and the wind is high." Could be any time in the next month, I guess,' I said, thinking we had heaps of time.

'Except,' Taid said, softly. 'There will be a full moon on Saturday—and the weather is changing.'

'It is? How can you tell?' The day was hot and still, without a breath of wind, and there wasn't a cloud in the sky, not even a little raggedy one.

'I read the signs, Catrin. The seagulls are flying inland, and the garden birds are hushed. Look at the beehive.'

I peeked nervously at the square, white hives under the honeysuckle hedge. I'd seen *The Swarm* and *Revenge of the Killer Bees* on a double bill at the movies with Kym, and it put me off bees-in-a-bunch for LIFE!

'I'm looking,' I said. 'I don't see bees.'

'Exactly!' Twm said. 'They're doing the bee equivalent of putting up the storm-shutters.'

'And there are other signs,' Taid went on. 'Too small and too many to bother you with. But trust me, the weather is changing.'

'So we have, like, two days to find this tanker and warn it?' I said, disbelievingly. 'Where do we start to find one ship out of millions?'

'Well,' Twm said. 'We know it is a Japanese tanker. If we go to the Library, we can look at Lloyd's List.'

'Lloyd who?' I asked.

'Lloyd's of London,' Twm said. 'The marine insurers. They publish a list of ships and their owners—and they also know where they are at any time.'

'So what are we waiting for?'

Pontpentre-dŵr didn't have a library, although a van came round with books twice a week, which I thought was real neat. But it meant we had to go to Cardigan to find one. A bus was due any minute, and Taid hurried us away to catch it.

'Shall I take the Signs?' I asked.

'Catrin, the Signs must go with you *everywhere*,' the old man said sternly. 'From now until you return them to the Sea-King's daughter, they must be with you day and night.'

The Librarian didn't want me to take my rucksack into the library. I guess she was kind of nervous I'd steal some books or something, because I didn't have any library card with me, and she'd only met me a couple or more times. Some people! She was *real* suspicious. Luckily Twm had his, and after I'd promised to open my bag and show her before we left, she let us inside.

We checked Lloyd's List, and found the owners of the *Kyoto Star*: Tokyo Imperial Shipping Line, and sure enough, it was heading our way.

'Gotcha,' I said, slamming the big book shut. 'And they have a London office, so all we need to do is call them up and tell them.' The minute I spoke, I got this picture of some telephonist stone-walling us, refusing to let us talk to anyone important enough to make that tanker stay in port someplace Saturday night. 'Not gonna work, is it, Twm?' I said, glumly. 'Even if we went to London to see the guy in charge, we'd still have to get past his secretary. Maybe if we used the Signs.'

Twm shook his head. 'We can only use them once, Catrin. We can't go about showing them to everyone like a—a—like a free pass to the zoo. We need to save them for the right time.'

'So,' I said. 'Where do we go from here?'

Twm rubbed his eyes, tiredly. 'I don't know. I just don't know.'

And then, suddenly, I did. 'I've got it!' I hollered. The

180

librarian gave me a disapproving glare, so I whispered instead. 'Mr Takahashi'll know how to find out! I know I can make *him* believe me. If I show him the Signs, then, then *he'll* call up the London people and make them believe him!'

Twm stared at me. 'Do you really think so? Will he believe you?'

'Sure!' I said, crossing my fingers behind my back. 'And I guess he's the only chance we've got.'

'Do you really believe that he's our only chance? Do your *bones* tell you, Catrin?'

I wasn't sure how I'd consult my bones, but I felt around inside my head. My brain said yes, my heart said yes, and I was mostly certain my bones did, too.

'Yeah, Twm,' I said, 'All my bits agree. Mr Takahashi is the right guy. Trust me.'

'Then we need to get you home, quickly,' Twm said.

I felt kind of relieved inside, as if all my loose ends had been neatly tied in bows, and my knots unravelled. All I had to do was go home and talk to Mr Takahashi, show him the Signs . . .

But.

I had sneaked out of the house before sun-up, left a note for my Mom, and not gone to Machynlleth. Was she gonna be mad? You got it.

When my Mom is real mad, the tip of her nose turns white. I sent Madoc in ahead of me, and he headed straight for his water dish. Mom was loading the dishwasher.

'Hi, Mom! I'm back. Did you have a good day? Where's Jake? Did Mrs Takahashi enjoy Machynlleth? What was the Centre like?' I gabbled, trying to fill that kitchen-full of frosty air with talk.

Mom straightened up and Looked at me. And yeah, the

tip of her nose was white. 'And what was so all-fired important you had to go sneaking out of the house before breakfast?' she asked icily. 'You knew perfectly well that I planned for you to go with us.'

I took a deep breath. 'Mom, I—'

'I hardly knew *what* to say to Mrs Takahashi. She'd been looking forward to having you along, and you didn't even have the courtesy to say you weren't going!' Mom steamrollered on. 'I was so *embarrassed*. I can't imagine what she thought of you. I thought your Dad and I had raised you with better manners!'

'I—'

'Well, young lady, what have you got to say for yourself?' I opened my mouth, but she hadn't finished yet. 'There is no excuse for your behaviour. I feel like grounding you forever, but since you have to go to the factory opening tomorrow for Dad's sake, I'm grounding you right after that—until you start school. Right at this moment, young lady, I'm *real* sorry we invited Twm to the opening. He's a bad influence on you. Mrs Gwynne-Davies told me all about *him*. She said he's not to be trusted, and I think she's right. But since we already invited him, he gets to come. But you do not run wild with him on that island any more. You stay put, on our beach, where I can see you. Mrs Gwynne-Davies said he's untrustworthy, and you aren't to have anything more to do with him.'

That was too much. 'Twm is not either untrustworthy!' I retorted. 'Twm is real nice, real kind, and my best friend in all the world. Please, you can't stop me seeing him, Mom! Not just because of something Mrs Gwynne-Davies said! She hates him! She's nothing but an old, an old—bat!' I finished.

'That is quite enough, Catrin Rhys Morgan,' Mom said

182

quietly. 'You can go to your room right this minute, and stay there. You may have your dinner on a tray. You can think of some way to apologise to Mrs Takahashi.'

'But Mom!' I pleaded.

'Not another word, Catrin. Go to your room.'

I *had* to speak to Mr Takahashi. 'Where's—'

'*Room*, Catrin. Go!'

I went.

I heard Jake come in a little later, and when he came upstairs to wash up for dinner, I stuck my head out of my room. 'Psst! I need to talk, Jake. Come on in my room.'

Jake tiptoed inside and I shut the door. 'Where're Mr and Mrs Takahashi?'

'Gone. And Dad.'

Gone? They couldn't have! 'Gone where?'

Jake borrowed my nail-file to scratch his name on his knee. Weird kid. 'They went up to London. The Ambassador is travelling down with them in the chopper tomorrow.'

'What Ambassador?'

'Oh, gee, Catrin. I know you kinda like Wales, but remember America? Huh? That big place we used to live? The American Ambassador, you pea-brain! He's opening the factory tomorrow, yeah?'

'Oh. *That* Ambassador. When will they be back?'

Jake put his headphones on and heavy metal reverberated tinnily from his walkman. He'd lost interest. 'What? Oh, tomorrow I guess: they're gonna go straight to the factory and Mom's gonna meet them there.' He clicked off his tape. 'She's real ticked off at you, Catty! Maybe she'll un-ground you about the time you get married, huh? If you're real lucky and can find some poor guy to take you on!' I scowled at him and he left.

Now I really had a problem. Back in Pittsburgh I had a telephone in my room, but here the only phone was in the kitchen. So even if Twm had had a house-phone I couldn't have called him without sneaking downstairs. And in Mom's present mood, if I did that and she caught me, I'd be dead meat. And the phone Twm used to call me was in a neat little red box outside the post office in the village.

Jake brought up some dinner on a tray, and even though I didn't feel hungry I ate it, because I had to keep my strength up. I didn't feel like sleeping, either, but I guess I did, despite the Earthstone in its box, the Sea-Harp, and the Sky-Egg sharing my duvet-space.

I woke up about two in the morning, partly because the box with the Earthstone was digging painfully into my ribs, partly because I was so darn thirsty! I wriggled away from the box, and lay with my eyes shut hoping the thirsty feeling would go. I didn't want to get out of bed and go down to the kitchen to get some juice. I could have drunk water from the bathroom, but I needed orange juice. This was an O.J. thirst, and nothing else would do. It didn't go. My throat got drier and drier, until I felt like I was, like, crawling through *Death Valley* looking for a drinks concession. I HAD TO HAVE ORANGE JUICE!

Eventually, I got out of bed, and padded downstairs in my p.j.'s and bare feet, sleep-walked into the kitchen and opened the ice-box. I sat at the kitchen table and gulped down a full glass, then re-filled it again and sipped more slowly. Half-asleep, it was a while before I realised that Madoc, shut in the outhouse overnight, was making a terrible fuss. I put on Dad's rubber boots, about fourteen sizes too big, which were standing outside the back door, and flapped out to hush him up. By the time I'd got there, he'd gone from barking to howling.

'Quiet, you dumb hound!' I hissed. 'It's only me, see?'
But he didn't stop. As soon as the door was open he rushed
past me, into the kitchen, and threw himself at the door to
the living room, skidding on the rag rug and scratching the
paintwork on the door. I was just about to speak to him real
sharp, when I kind of realised that this was not Madoc-type
behaviour. I crouched down and held his muzzle, holding
him close to calm him, and his little body trembled
violently.

'What is it, Madoc?' I put my ear to the kitchen door
and listened. Apart from Dad, snoring (he could snore for
the U.S.A. at Olympic standard!) the house was silent.
Madoc wrenched himself free and hurtled back into the
outhouse, this time throwing himself at the door into the
garden, again barking wildly.

Scared he was going to wake Mom and Dad, I opened
the back door and let him out into the garden. He rushed to
the gate, and I ran after, arriving there just in time to see
the brake lights of a large, dark car come on as it crossed
the bridge to the village.

'There, you dumb bunny!' I said, still trying to calm
him. 'Just some guy necking with his girl at the beach, I
guess. Don't make such a fuss, Madoc.'

But he still wouldn't calm down. He was getting
hysterical now, and was hurling himself so hard at the
kitchen door that I opened it, afraid he'd hurt himself (or
break the door!). He squeezed through the gap before it
was fully open, yelping as he caught his ribs in passing—
and up the stairs into my room. I followed him, and found
him scrabbling at the duvet.

I pulled back the Snoopy cover: the Earthstone, the Sea-
Harp and the Sky-Egg were gone.

CHAPTER TWENTY-TWO

I sat on the bed, feeling sick. Just when I'd gotten all the Signs, I'd left them lying about for the Others to get in and steal them. I thought about getting dressed and rushing over to Twm's, but if I'm honest, I didn't want to tell him how damn *dumb* I'd been. I knew I had to get them back. It was dark outside, and windy, but the moon was almost full.

I remembered the car tail-lights. Humphreys was safely locked up, and so was Mrs Prosser, which only left Mrs Gwynne-Davies. I thought of her bent little-old-lady frame, and wondered whether she could drive that big car. I remembered Taid saying that there were always four Spoilers—maybe the fourth one, whoever it was, had driven, and Mrs Gwynne-Davies had gotten in and stolen the Signs while I was downstairs. But how did they know I'd be in the kitchen, drinking juice, and not in my bed guarding the Signs? Maybe *they'd* given me that thirst—if we could give them poison-ivy, I guess they could manage a simple O.J. attack. While I was thinking, I got dressed in a dark sweater, jeans and sneakers, and put a warm jacket on over the top. I decided, much as I hated to have to do it, I had to tell Twm and Taid what had happened. They'd know what to do. Madoc, now he'd made me understand, sat patiently beside me. We crept downstairs and out of the house through the outhouse. I tried not to think what my Mom would say if she woke up and found me gone!

I set off, running at a steady jog. I'd gone about half a mile when I realised I wasn't heading for Twm's house, but away from it. I stopped, turned round, and began to run back—then realised I'd turned round again, and was heading away from Taid and Twm. SOMETHING was pushing me in the direction it wanted me to go! But who? I thought about it as I jogged, and then decided it probably wasn't the Spoilers. If they'd been able to make me run towards them, I guess they'd just have made me bring the Signs with me, wouldn't they?

Still and all, it would have been kinda nice to know where I was going! I was running real well—I wasn't out of breath at all, and I felt like I could go on for miles. The moon lit the road, so it was almost as bright as daylight, but the sides of the road were real dark, shadowy and majorly scary, so I ran straight down the middle! A huge pair of black wrought iron gates loomed up on the left, set between two stone pillars, each topped by a big, ugly, threatening-looking statue of a bird. The right-hand pillar bore a sign—'Nant-Gwynne Hall'.

The gates swung open—not making any screechy noises, or clangs, but *real quiet*, like they were expecting me. It looked like I had to go between the big birds— which had nothing at all in common with the one on *Sesame Street*!

The gravel driveway crunched under my feet, so I switched to the grassy edges. I didn't like to be close to the scary trees, but at least no one could see me in the shadows. The drive curved, disappearing behind the house, a huge dark shape against the trees. In back of the house I saw Mrs Gwynne-Davies's big limousine parked next to a garage. I touched the hood—the engine was still warm. The house was dark, except for a glow from behind a reddish curtain on the ground floor. I crept across, keeping to the grass when I could, wincing every time I hit gravel. I crouched below the window, then poked my head up. Through a crack in the curtains I could see a strand of white hair, a great beak of a nose—Mrs Gwynne-Davies. I could hear voices, but not what they were saying. Somehow I had to get inside.

Boy, oh, boy. Sneaking out of the house, breaking and entering. I'd end up in jail for sure, if Mom didn't kill me first. I went round to the front of the house where there were four ground floor windows, all of them shut. Round the corner, though, was a large pair of patio doors. I slithered up and tried the handle: the door slid silently across, and I slipped inside leaving it slightly open for a real fast exit—if necessary! My nose was right up against a dusty curtain, and I could feel a sneeze coming. I held my nose and prayed for it to go away, because if I sneezed now, I'd probably blow my brains out my ears . . . I do real good sneezes.

At last, it stopped tickling, and I crept out from behind the curtain, waiting a while for my eyes to get accustomed to the darkness of the room. I put my hand on Madoc's head and whispered at him to stay. Obediently the pup sat, silent and still.

I wished I'd thought to bring a flashlight with me. I could see the dim outline of a big table in the centre of the room, surrounded by chairs, so I made an amazing deduction and decided I was in the dining room (intelligent, huh?). A bar of light shone under the door across the room, so I crept towards it, sliding my feet on the floor so as not to trip on anything I couldn't see, and putting my hands out so that I wouldn't bump into furniture and stuff. I reached the door safely and silently opened it. Beyond was a hallway with a telephone on a table, a tall closet, and three doors leading off. One was open into darkness, but the other two were shut, so I crept up and listened at each one until I heard voices behind one. I peered through the key-hole. I could see the back of two

188

wing chairs, and a low table, the Troll's white hair like thin cotton-candy over the top of one of the chairs, but in the other, all I could see was a slim white hand, fingernails long and painted dark red—horrible nails, like talons. But on the table, all together, were the Sea-Harp, the Sky-Egg, and the box containing the Earthstone. The Sky-Egg looked dull, and kind of depressed, as if it didn't like to be there. How could I get them? I had none of Taid's powder, Twm was miles away. It was just ordinary old me.

I'd forgotten Madoc. From right outside the window of the room I was peering into, came his puppy-yap. Mrs Gwynne-Davies said, 'That's the ginger brat's dog—she's here! Quickly, if we catch her we can make the old man give us Humphreys and Prosser. Quick, you fool!'

I reacted real fast—terror has that effect on me! I shot into the tall closet in the hall just as the door to the room burst open, and feet pounded past towards the front door. Once the feet had retreated, I opened the door and peeked out. The hall was empty, the front door open.

I shot into the room and rushed to get the Signs. I looked around for something to carry them in: a supermarket shopper lay on the floor, and I scooped the Signs inside. The Sky-Egg flickered with turquoise light as I touched it, as if it recognised me.

Madoc was still yapping out front as I slipped out the side door carrying the Signs, across the lawn and into the trees. I tried to whistle, but my lips were so dry with nerves nothing came out except a huffing noise.

So I pitched my voice real low, and called 'Madoc. Come on, boy!'

Instantly the barking stopped, and a small shape shot round the corner of the house towards me. Clutching the plastic bag to my chest, I pounded down the grass verge

189

towards the gates, trying to put as much distance between me and the Spoilers as I could. Someone spotted me and shouted, and shortly after I heard a car engine start up. I was through the iron gates before it caught up with me, but the headlights shone down the road, and forced me back into the trees. I shoved the bag under my jacket, in case the white plastic reflected and betrayed me, and wondered what to do next. I was real scared, because I knew they would stop at nothing to catch me. The car slowed at the gates, and Mrs Gwynne-Davies got out, waved her arms at the stone birds, and shouted several long words I couldn't understand.

And the birds took off! Creakily, stiffly, they lumbered off their gateposts and into the night sky, their wings whistling through the air, heading towards me. I shrank back against a tree, keeping real still as the birds came closer. I wished I was miles away, safe in bed.

The huge, black shapes flapped blackly down the road towards me, and I shut my eyes, not wanting to believe what I was seeing. They cawed, loudly, like giant rooks, crashing through branches, swooping, darting, looking for ME! I guess I thought my last hour had come. Then the car, its headlamps on full beam, came slowly down the road, and stopped a few yards from where I was hid. I could see it, clearly. One of the rear windows slid down, and Mrs Gwynne-Davies's voice said, 'I know that you are there, girl. We have the Signs. You may as well give up. We shall win, I promise.' Then she laughed. It wasn't a nice laugh. I clenched my teeth. Boy, was she gonna be mad when she discovered the Signs were gone!

Then I noticed Madoc had my jeans-leg between his teeth and was determinedly tugging me backwards. I had to go with him, or fall over, so I went. I backed into the wood, not taking my eyes off the horrible birds, deeper and deeper into the darkness. When they had disappeared down the road, ahead of the big, black car, I turned, and followed Madoc into the depths of the wood. So long as I kept the white blob on the end of his tail in sight, I knew I was safe, and I followed that waving flag for miles! I didn't know where I was headed, but I trusted Madoc.

I wanted to go home real bad—but I knew that that was the first place the Spoilers would look when they didn't find me on the road. Once out of the wood, Madoc led me around the edges of fields, keeping in hedge-shadows so that we couldn't be seen from above. We slithered past sleepy cows and sheep, and once we disturbed a fox flickering like a flame along the border of a hedge. Suddenly I recognised the outskirts of Pontpentre-dŵr, and the back of Taid's cottage. I pushed through the hedge, heedless of scratches, and pounded on the back door. Overhead a window opened, and Twm's sleepy voice called 'Who is it?'

'Me, Twm!' I called. 'Open the door, quick!'

Twm, wearing real snazzy red p.j.'s, opened the door seconds later, and let me in. By the time Taid had put on his robe and come down, the kettle was boiling on the hob and me and my white plastic bag were sitting in the high-back wooden chair. Now I was safe I shook like jell-o, and my teeth chattered like castanets! Taid patted my hand and gave me a hot drink, and sipping it helped calm me.

I explained what had happened. 'I needed a drink and left the Signs upstairs,' I said. 'I can not believe I *did* that! I've gotten them back—but they sent their gateposts after me!'

I guess it took a while for Taid and Twm to unravel my story—I wasn't making a whole lot of sense. Once they

191

had it straight, though, Taid said, 'The Spoilers will keep trying right up until the last minute, Catrin. I should have realised that this might happen. You'd better stay here for the rest of the night,' he suggested. 'You'll be safe here.'

I shook my head. 'Uh-huh. No way! If Mom finds out I've been out again, she'll turn me into ground beef and then barbecue me! I've got to get home, Taid, real fast.' I thought about going out in the dark again. What if Mrs Gwynne-Davies—who must know by know that I had the Signs—was waiting? And the awful birds . . .

Twm read my expression. 'Wait until just before dawn, then,' he suggested. 'Then I'll go with you, make sure you get home safely, and you can creep in before your mother wakes up.'

Taid gave me the last two packs of powder. 'As soon as you are home, sprinkle yourself and the Signs with a little bit of it. That will keep you safe until you get to the factory opening. Then you must get to see the man—Mr Takahashi, isn't it?—and use the Signs to stop this disaster happening. Only you can do it, Catrin. If I could, or Twm, we would, but you are the Sea-Girl. And when the powder is gone, you have only the Signs. Use them well, Catrin.'

'I will,' I promised. 'Still and all, if I use one of the powders when I get home, I've got the other one just in case anything happens at the opening, don't I?'

I crept back into the house just as the dawn chorus was beginning, so loud that I was kind of scared it might wake Mom and she'd catch me. But I got safely back into my room in good time, and even managed a doze before Mom sent Jake to wake me.

CHAPTER TWENTY-THREE

Mom was slightly less mad at breakfast. The white had gone from the end of her nose, but she was still not in the kind of mood to josh around.

We had to be at the new factory by noon, and Twm was supposed to come over and ride with us. When he arrived, looking real smart in a suit, Mom was polite, but not friendly. He looked at me behind her back and raised his eyebrows, and I pulled a face. Mom made him sit up front in the car with her, and Jake and me got to sit in back. I knew there was no way Mom would let me bring my rucksack, so I hid it in the trunk of the car when she wasn't looking.

I didn't get a chance to talk with Twm until we arrived, when Mom had to go find the other V.I.P.s—Mayors, and Councilmen, Sirs and Members of the British Parliament, people like that, and left us with Jake.

'Where are the Signs?' Twm asked, anxiously.

'In the trunk of the car,' I explained. 'I'll go get 'em now.'

'I don't know what you guys are talking about,' Jake said, 'but you ain't gonna get nothin' from the car, Catty. Mom took the keys, remember?'

My face fell. Then I remembered Taid's last little packet of powder, and we rushed outside to sprinkle it on the lock. Twm slung the rucksack on his back—if Mom saw *me* carrying it she'd freak.

Dad, the Ambassador (Mr Winfield Tate Winfield III of Boston, Massachussets) and the Takahashis arrived—we saw them from the window of the staff restaurant, which was where all us not-quite-V.I.P. folks had to stay for lunch while the real important people ate in the boardroom. I wasn't hungry. The Signs were in the bag on Twm's back, I was there, the Takahashis were there—only I couldn't get at them, was all.

Outside, the sky was changing, filling with rainclouds, and the trees outside the window were swaying and bending in the gathering wind. I munched on a fingernail.

Jake, his mouth full of roast turkey, dug me in the ribs with his elbow. 'You'll catch it if Mom sees you bitin' your nails,' he advised. 'Say, this turkey's good.'

'You're the turkey, Jake!' I snapped. I felt so helpless— there was nothing I could do, no way to get out of this chattering, munching crowd of freeloaders and get Mr Takahashi on his own. Then I remembered Dad's secretary, Mrs Williams. If I could get to her, she'd help me find Dad. And where Dad was, of course, so was Mr Takahashi.

I told Jake I was gonna show Twm where the bathroom was, but he was so busy trying to eat Takahashi Electronics (Wales) out of turkey and potato salad he hardly noticed. I knew more or less where Mrs Williams's office was. If she wasn't in it, maybe I could find someone to go give her a message.

Twm and me slipped out of the staff restaurant and slithered down the hallway, like a pair of movie spies, peering round corners before we went round them. Mrs Williams's room was right next to Dad's, and when we reached it my spirits rose—I could see a dark shape at the desk through the frosted glass.

'She's there, Twm!' I said, and flung open the door. 'Hi, Mrs Wil . . . Oh.'

A strange blonde-haired woman with too much orangey make-up and long red fingernails sat at the desk.

194

'Um—hi!' I began. 'I'm looking for Mrs Williams. Is she about, please?'

The woman stood up. She was real tall, and there was something I didn't like a whole lot about her smile. It had, like, too many teeth in it.

'Mrs Williams is sick. I'm Miss Critchett, her replacement.'

'Mrs Williams is *sick?*' I found that kind of hard to believe—Mrs Williams would rather die than let Dad handle Opening Day without her! 'What's wrong?'

'Food poisoning,' she said, then smiled her unpleasant smile. Twm suddenly grabbed me real tight above the elbow, and was pulling me backwards. I dragged my arm away. 'I need to see my Dad real bad,' I said.

'And who might your Dad be?' She had nasty thin eyebrows, and she raised them.

'My Dad's David Rhys Morgan—the Managing Director. Could you go find him for me, please?'

The girl came round the desk. 'How do I know you're telling the truth? Anyone can fake an American accent. And security is very tight, because of the Ambassador. We can't let just anyone wander about.'

I started to lose my temper. 'I'm not asking you to let us wander about. I'm asking you to find my Dad. Please.'

The girl examined her red talons and then pressed a button on the wall. 'I don't think so.'

Twm grabbed me again and this time succeeded in hauling me backwards into the hallway. 'Come *on*, you dimwit!' he hissed. 'She's a Spoiler, can't you tell?'

I stared at the girl. I guess a little light bulb went on over my head. The red talons, y'know? Twm, dragging me, streaked down the hallway, but the girl didn't follow. We reached the end and swung round the corner thinking we'd escaped. Straight into the arms of a pair of security guards.

'Gotcha!' one of them panted, grabbing me, and the other grabbed Twm, twisting his arm up behind his back. The rucksack containing the Signs fell to the floor, and I just managed to hook one of the straps and haul it with me as the gorilla dragged me off.

'What do you guys think you're doing?' I said, as haughtily as I could with my arms held tightly. 'How dare you! I'm the Managing Director's daughter, and I demand that you take me to him.'

The guard holding Twm opened the door of a small, dark room, little more than a large closet. 'Maybe later, love. Right now we can't take any chances, what with the Ambassador here. Once he's gone, then maybe you can see your Dad—if he is your Dad, which he probably isn't, 'cos if he *was* your Dad, you'd be with 'im, wouldn't you? Not sneaking around with this one 'ere.'

Twm was shoved in, and me after him. The door was closed and we heard a key turn in the lock. At least they put on the light, because there were no windows. One of the guards stayed outside—we could hear him singing to himself, kinda flat for a Welshman.

'*Now* what do we do?' I said, slumping to the office floor. 'The powder's all gone. I guess we're finished. We blew it, Twm.'

Twm sat beside me, his head down. 'I think you're right, Catrin.'

I hefted the rucksack, glumly. 'Still and all, I guess we've got the Signs.'

'And a fat lot of good those are going to do us stuck in here,' Twm said.

Then it hit me. 'Twm! We've got the signs!'

He looked at me real patient. 'And we're stuck in a cupboard with them!' he pointed out.

I raised my eyes to the ceiling. I didn't often get to score points. 'And-one-of-the-Signs-is-the-Earthstone, Twm!' I explained patiently. 'Everything back to its source, remember? No stone standing one on another, remember?'

Twm got slowly to his feet. A grin spread. 'Oh, Catrin. You're right! Quick—get it out!'

My fingers were stiff and clumsy, but eventually I managed to fumble the buckles undone and take out the iron box with the Earthstone. I unpacked it, and it lay on my hand, glinting in the dim overhead electric light. 'What shall we do with it?' I asked. 'Shall I zap the door?'

'With a security guard outside? No chance. No, it has to be the walls.' We looked around us. The walls between the store-closet and the adjoining rooms were made of a sort of woody stuff—what we could see of them behind the packs of paper and boxes of ball-point pens and stuff.

I put the Earthstone back in its iron box so it didn't start without us, and then, as quietly as we could, we emptied the shelves on the wall furthest away from the door. When the shelves were bare, I laid the Earthstone against the back wall.

For a second nothing happened, and then the wallboard began first to crumble away, then to reassemble itself, sending out twigs, leaves, and branches. A large brown root snaked down through a gap in a floorboard. I put the Earthstone back in its box, fast, before it demolished the factory completely. The growing tree left a gap big enough for us to crawl through. Twm went through first, and I squirmed through after him into an office, with a computer terminal on a desk, and one door leading to the hallway, one to another, bigger office. We crept silently into the big office, at the far end of which was another door which opened around the corner of the corridor from where the security guard sat—guarding an empty stationery closet! Oh, and a tree, putting out leaves, on the back wall . . .

Twm stuck his nose round, real careful, then slipped out. We stood in the deserted hallway, listening. We could hear a voice, somewhere, giving what seemed to be a speech, and then a burst of loud clapping. 'The opening ceremony's started!' I whispered, and we headed for the applause, which was coming from the foyer of the main building.

CHAPTER TWENTY-FOUR

Everybody had crowded in, and Mr and Mrs Takahashi and Mom and Dad stood beside a very tall, heavy-set man who was about to unveil something covered by the Stars-and-Bars and the Welsh dragon flags, one draped over each side.

'It gives me great pleasure to be here in your beautiful little country, and I'm real honoured to declare Takahashi Electronics (Wales) well and truly open!'

Flashbulbs popped, everybody clapped and cheered, and the big guy pulled the ribbon to uncover a plaque. I clapped real loud, then remembered we had a job to do. Dad was ushering the Ambassador and the Takahashis through the double doors at the back of the foyer, back into the boardroom elevator ready for the press conference.

'Come on, Catrin,' Twm said, and we struggled through the throng towards the elevator doors just as they slid closed. I got my elbow inside, shoved real hard, and the two of us tumbled in on top of the Ambassador.

'Catrin!' my mother said, in a real scandalised voice. '*What* are you doing?'

Mr Takahashi didn't look real pleased, either, and my Dad just looked kinda horrified. If this didn't go right, I was ground beef.

The Ambassador scowled, and slithered behind a large bodyguard-type guy with dark glasses (I ask you, in an elevator!').

'Mr Ambassador Sir, my daughter Catrin, and her friend Twm,' Dad said. He smiled in a wishy-washy kind of way, but his eyes were saying 'I'm gonna KILL somebody for this!'

Twm and I solemnly shook hands with the Ambassador, who came out from behind his bodyguard.

Mr Takahashi looked distant. 'Whatever Catrin wants, David, I hope it's extremely important.' That was bad—he wasn't talking directly to me.

'Mr Takahashi,' I pleaded. 'I really, really need to talk to you about something. It's majorly, majorly important.'

Mr Takahashi was still pretending I wasn't there. 'David,' he turned to my father, 'I suggest you escort your daughter and her friend downstairs.'

The elevator doors slid open, and the Ambassador and Mr Takahashi stepped out. Dad turned to grab me. His face was scarlet. He was *not* a happy puppy! This wasn't gonna work.

'*Please*, Mr Takahashi,' I called after his disappearing back, 'please, please, listen to me?'

'No, you listen to ME, young lady—' Dad began, and I really thought we'd blown it.

And then Mrs Takahashi spoke up. 'Just a moment, Ito,' she said, firmly. 'And Mr Ambassador, please, wait. I've gotten to know this young lady quite well, and she certainly wouldn't interrupt something so important to her Dad unless she had a real good reason. I guess maybe we should listen to her?'

Dad had lumps of hair sticking up in clumps, and my Mom was steaming, boiling mad. And yeah, the end of her nose was white. She started to say 'No, I—' but Mrs Takahashi kind of steamrollered everyone into the boardroom, waved at the assembled photographers, and sat us in a corner.

'Just as soon as the press guys are out of here, you two can tell us what gives. OK, honey?' And she winked at me.

My knees felt weak with relief, and despite the look my

Mom gave me, I felt that we might make it after all. Twm and me sat on the edge of our chairs until the last flashbulb had popped and the TV guys had wandered off to take pictures of the factory and talk to some of the staff.

When the doors had closed behind them, all the grown-ups turned on us: Winfield Tate Winfield III, Mr and Mrs Takahashi, and Mom and Dad. None of them looked too pleased with us—although Mrs Takahashi maybe *might* be on our side, just a bit!

'Now,' Dad began, and cleared his throat. Mr Takahashi was still real steaming mad, I could tell, but luckily Dad knew I wouldn't behave this bad for no reason. Mom, though, was still feeling mad at me for disappearing yesterday, and looked as if she might ground me forever and then some, and I guess right then she believed that I was capable of about anything, including mid-air hi-jacking and bank robbery!

I opened my mouth to start explaining, but Twm spoke up first. I felt a bit mad and kind of relieved at the same time, because I sure didn't know what I was about to say.

Twm said, 'I know it looks bad, and it's going to be very difficult for you to believe us, but if you could just listen, and try really, really hard, I hope you'll understand why we've done this.'

Twm began with the legends, and after looking kind of impatient for a minute or two, Mr Winfield got kinda caught up in the stories and even Mr Takahashi lost his tight-mouthed look. Mom and Dad were still embarrassed—but at last even they started to listen. Twm was telling the stories so well that they couldn't help it. He got to the end of the legends, and then told about me finding the Sky Egg.

'You remember, Mom?' I chipped in. 'I got the Egg

from the back room that didn't exist when we went back to look. Only nobody but me could see how real special it was. And then I found the Sea-Harp, and then the Earthstone, and yesterday I couldn't go with you to Machynlleth because Taid said Twm and me had to find Merlin's mirror to find out what the danger is.'

'Catrin, this is such a *tale*!' Mom said. 'If you're trying to excuse your bad behaviour with this—this—nonsense I'll—But surely even you wouldn't ruin Dad's day like this.'

'No, Mom!' I said.

'No Mom, nothing,' she went on, 'I'm still not convinced.' The tip of her nose seemed slightly less white. I crossed my fingers behind my back, and Hoped.

Twm held up his hand, like a traffic cop—and miraculously, there was silence.

'Please believe us, Mrs Morgan. Honestly, Catrin is the Sea-Girl, and she has the Signs. And unless we can prevent it, there will be a terrible accident. According to Merlin's mirror, an oil tanker will collide with a passenger ferry in Cardigan Bay in a great storm on the night of the full moon, and people will die, and the oil from the tanker will pollute the coast—even as far as your Toll House and my Island, but with your help we can stop it happening. There's a full moon tonight. And a storm is brewing. Mrs Takahashi—think of the seals!'

Mom was still not convinced. 'What storm? The weather's wonderful! OK, so maybe there's gonna be a full moon, but—what storm?'

Mr Takahashi let out a long sigh. 'Mrs Morgan, I think your anger with Catrin is affecting your judgment. Look out of the window, dear lady. There is certainly bad weather on the way.'

Outside, the wind whipped the trees, and the grass in the fields alongside the factory was lying flat as if a giant hand was pressing down, and they and the parking lot next the factory were dotted with seagulls. The sky was filled with more gulls swooping inland, and over the sea, the sky was an ominous yellowish grey. Thunder rumbled in the distance.

'So maybe there's gonna be a bit of a storm,' Winfield Tate Winfield III said. 'But are these kids claiming they can see into the future? Come on! This is the twentieth century!' He stuck his hands in his pockets and rocked on his heels. 'Two boats? A passenger ferry and a bulk oil-tanker? No names? No details? Aah. This is just kids, attention-getting. They need strict handling, Mr Morgan. I confess, I'm scandalised an American kid could behave like this. Can't speak for the natives, I guess, but no kid of mine would behave this bad.'

'The name of the tanker is the *Kyoto Star*,' Twm said quietly. 'It is due in Milford Haven tonight, unless it is blown off course by the storm. Catrin is telling the truth, Mr Winfield.' (Did his Mom call him 'Winnie'? 'Fieldie'? Or something worse!)

'What are you kids *talking* about?' Dad groaned, pushing his fingers through his hair. 'Mr Takahashi, I can't apologise enough.'

Mr Takahashi held up a hand and Dad shut up. 'My wife,' he said, and smiled at her. 'My wife is a wonderful and sensitive woman. I trust her judgment. So, my dear. What do you think?'

Mrs Takahashi kicked off her shoes and wriggled her toes in the carpet. She stared at her pink piggies for a minute, and then looked up at me, her head on one side like a small bird, then at Twm.

'I believe them, Ito. But Catrin—you say you have the Sea-Girl's Signs. What are they?'

I glanced at Twm, then I opened the rucksack and took out, first, the Sky Egg and placed it on the boardroom table where the polished wood reflected its blue glimmer. From the expression on their faces, Mom and Dad still didn't see anything but an old stone. Next I removed the Sea-Harp, and placed it beside the Egg, its silvery strings sending a faint ripple of music into the silence. Last, I got out the Earthstone, and put it, in its iron box, beside the other two Signs. I guess the boardroom table busting out with twigs and leaves might have convinced them, but it also might have kinda distracted them!

'A shell, a stone egg, and a large pebble,' Mom said. 'Are these supposed to be your Signs? Hah!'

'Look!' Mrs Takahashi said.

CHAPTER TWENTY-FIVE

We looked. The shell started it—I guess the Sea-Harp was the first Sign in the Legends, so it was right that it kind of led the way.

It started to, like *glow*, as if a bright candle was inside. The creamy white outside took on the pinkness of the inside, and as it grew brighter and brighter, the harpstrings began to vibrate, and suddenly music filled the room. It wasn't ordinary music, either—it was like, like—oh, gee, it was *indescribable,* OK? It got inside my head and made me think of long, empty sea-shores, and the sound the wind made when it whistled sand up around your ears, and sea-birds crying, and somehow even a flutey, tinkly sound, like shell wind-chimes. At the ripple of sound from the Sea-Harp everyone in the room, except me and Twm, froze to the spot—like Grandmother's footsteps, you know?

Next, the Sky-Egg started up. It, too, glowed from inside, like the Sea-Harp, and pulsated, and sent out a high, clear note like crystal bells. When the Earthstone joined in, it made the sound of mighty waters booming, deep and echo-ey, kind of vibrating all the way up from my toes to the top of my head. The jaggedy, sparkly rock in the middle of the smooth stone flashed rainbow fire on the boardroom walls.

I looked at Mom and Dad, rooted to the spot. Mr and Mrs Takahashi had identical amazed expressions, and Mr Winfield Tate Winfield, United States Ambassador, was frozen with his mouth wide open.

It got better yet. On the wall of the boardroom—the Sky Egg was acting like one of those real old-fashioned kind of movie projectors, you know?—a huge mirror took shape, misty at first, then clearing.

'Merlin's mirror,' Twm explained. The eyes of all the grown-ups in the room swivelled towards the wall as the mirror obligingly replayed the tanker/ferry accident. It still made me shiver, even though I knew what was gonna happen. It ended with a cormorant, its feathers clogged with oil, struggling vainly to lift itself out of the cloying stuff slithering thickly on the surface of the sea . . . As the pictures faded Twm rippled the strings of the Sea-Harp and the Ambassador, Mom, Dad and the Takahashis were un-frozen.

It was Dad who broke the stuned silence. 'OK,' he said, 'I guess we believe you. Question is, what can we do about it? Seems to me, if it's gonna happen, it's gonna happen.'

'No, Dad,' I said. 'Maybe if Mr Takahashi telephones the *Kyoto Star's* owners, maybe they can tell it to turn back to—oh, I don't know—what port? Liverpool, maybe?'

'Could Liverpool handle a bulk oil tanker?' Dad asked Mr Takahashi. He shrugged.

'If it can't, then maybe it can just be delayed enough to miss the bad weather. Maybe it could run inshore a bit and anchor, something like that, ride out the storm,' Twm suggested. 'Only, we've got to try, Sir. Please? We've got to keep that tanker out of Cardigan Bay. You didn't see the last disaster, just outside the Haven, but I was there, and I remember it in my nightmares. We can't let it happen again.'

Mr Takahashi rubbed his jaw, thoughtfully. 'Honey,' Mrs Takahashi said, sharply. 'You have to give it a try.'

'Yes, dear,' my father's boss said, meekly, and reached for the telephone. 'What's your secretary's name, David?'

'Mrs W—. No. Mrs Williams is sick. The temp's name is Miss Critchett.'

'No!' Twm and I said, both together. 'You can't ask her. She's a Spoiler.'

'A *what*?' Dad asked, mystified, but Mr Takahashi put the phone down.

'I think I know about Spoilers,' he said, mysteriously. 'In America and in Japan, we also have Spoilers. Often, in high places.'

'So what do we do now?' Twm asked, frowning. 'Can't we dial the company's number on the boardroom phone?'

'We could,' Mr Takahashi said, thoughtfully. 'But I think Miss Critchett might be listening in.'

'So, what?' Twm asked. 'Time is running out, Sir.'

Dad pushed his hair back some more, and Mom looked worried. Mr Winfield cleared his throat. 'If you have the number,' he volunteered, smiling kind of shyly, 'I have a mobile.'

I leapt upon him and ripped the phone out of his hand, passing it to Mr Takahashi, who within seconds was asking Directory Enquiries for the number of the Tokyo Imperial Shipping Line, and minutes after that, was speaking in rapid Japanese to someone on the other end.

From the half-conversation we heard, he was getting kind of teed off with the guy, who wasn't listening so good, and in the end he stood up real straight, and barked something that sounded like an order into the phone. Mrs Takahashi winced.

'Ito, really!' she said, when he handed back the phone to the Ambassador. 'Such language! It's a real good thing these young folks don't speak Japanese.'

Mr Takahashi scowled. 'Stupid man wouldn't listen.'

Mrs Takahashi shook her head. 'Still, Ito. To be so rude—.'

Mr Takahashi grinned. 'It did the job, though. The *Kyoto Star* is under orders to turn back into the nearest deepwater port that can handle it. In any event, it will be nowhere near Cardigan Bay tonight.'

'Your Island is safe, Twm,' Mrs Takahashi said, softly. 'And your seals, and your dolphins, and the seabirds. All safe.'

I felt a grin spread across my face. We'd done it! The tanker would be safe in port, there would be no hole, no oil, and no polluted seabirds, seals, dolphins—or Island. I put the Signs back in my rucksack, and Twm shuffled his feet. 'Thanks, Mr Takahashi,' he said eventually. 'I'm very sorry we upset your Opening Day.'

Mr Takahashi smiled, shaking his head. 'It wasn't too upset—and if such a disaster had happened it would have knocked the Opening out of the headlines anyway. And it certainly isn't a day I'm likely to forget, young man! It's a pity we couldn't get all your Signs and their special effects on camera for tonight's news—now *that* would have given us some publicity!'

'Kind of funny you should say that, Ito!' Mr Winfield said, rubbing his hands together. 'It just so happens that I own this little TV station back home—WTWTV.' He put his arm round my shoulders and gave me a friendly squeeze. 'Hows about it, young lady? Hows about you come on camera for my TV station and tell your story? My viewers just love anything weird and wonderful—and it don't come any weirder or wonderfuller than what you kids just did!'

'Ah,' Twm said, thoughtfully. 'I'm really sorry, Mr Winfield, but—'

He stepped in front of the big man, and looked deep into his eyes. 'Mr Winfield. Look at me, please, if you will. Mr Winfield, NOTHING HAPPENED HERE TODAY. Nothing at all. It was just a normal, ordinary, routine factory opening. Nothing else. Very boring. Do you understand?'

Mr Winfield's face got kinda relaxed, and he looked faintly puzzled. 'Gotcha. Yeah. Nothing happened. Right. OK.' He yawned, and seemed to fall asleep standing up. Mr and Mrs Takahashi exchanged glances. 'I hope you aren't going to do that to us!' Mrs Takahashi said sternly. 'We want to keep our memories. We won't ever talk about them, I promise—but we would like to keep them, if you please.'

Twm grinned. 'Oh, I think that'll be all right, Mrs Takahashi. After all, you are a Sea-Person. You'll keep the secret.'

'And my Mom and Dad!' I added.

'Hmm,' Mom said. I was kind of glad to see the end of her nose was quite normal again. 'I'm not sure what happened here this afternoon—but I guess it kinda explains how you've been behaving lately young lady!'

'It does, Mom,' I agreed. Then I remembered. 'Am I still grounded until I grow apples?'

'I guess not.'

'Great.' My tummy gurgled. 'Say. Could we go downstairs and get something to eat? I'm starved.'

Later that evening we all sat, including Twm, who was back in Mom's good favours, and watched the early evening TV reports of the opening. Right at the end of the programme, the weathergirl showed us a mass of tightly packed isobars, and talked about ninety-miles-an-hour winds, and mentioned this bulk oil tanker that had turned

209

back into port because of threatened bad weather . . . She said the best place for us was right where we were, safe at home, and I had to agree.

Wind howled around the Toll House, and rain rattled on the windows. I reached for another chocolate brownie, stretching my toes out ecstatically to the fire in the hearth. I felt kind of smug, you know? Inside, in the warm, with a howling gale outside, and chocolate fudge brownies. What a real awful night to be caught at sea. Still and all, at least we managed to save the tanker from colliding with . . .

'Oh, shoot!' I bellowed, leaping out of my chair, scaring Madoc stiff and scattering brownie crumbs all over the rugs. 'Twm! We forgot the ferryboat!'

Twm turned pale, leapt out of his chair and headed for the telephone.

'Who you gonna call?' I asked, following him, and Jake, coming downstairs with a computer game in his hand, added '*Ghostbusters*!' automatically. I was so worried we might have blown it, I didn't even tell him to hush up.

'Coastguard,' Twm said, briefly, and punched the nine button three times, real fast. It's a good thing he got to the phone before me, because I'd have wasted time dialling nine-eleven, which is emergency services in the States.

Twm lied some when he got put through to the Coastguard—he said he'd picked up a radio message from a ferryboat out of Fishguard which had lost engine power and was drifting in Cardigan Bay. It didn't matter—the Coastguard went ahead and organized the rescue anyway—though they were kind of puzzled next day when they heard that the ferry's radio had been out of order and it hadn't sent out a may-day call! There were close on three hundred people on board, and the next day's news had shots of pale green people trooping down the gangplank after being towed into port. They were real sea-sick—but at least they were alive!

*   *   *

Twm called for me early next morning, while I was still wearing my p.j.'s and eating breakfast. I hastily dressed in denim cut-offs and a sweatshirt—but I had a swimsuit underneath, and a T-shirt in my rucksack underneath the Signs. The storm had blown itself out, and the fresh-painted morning was slightly chill after the night's downpour. The sand was scoured flat and clean, and the trees on the rim of the beach shivered drops of rainwater. The sea was still faintly choppy, and the tide had left strands of green weed and driftwood, like a beachcomber's collage, all along the high-water mark.

We were going to give back the Signs, but I wasn't sure how I felt about it. They'd served their purpose, I guess, and it was right that they should be returned. To be real honest, I'd be glad to be rid of the Earthstone—I felt kind of uncomfortable carrying that around, in case it worked out some way to return the iron in the box to iron ore, while I was asleep some night, and I woke up in a forest that had once been my fourpost bed surrounded by a heap of rubble that had once been the Toll House!

'They have to go back to her, Catrin.'

'I know, Twm. Only—being the Sea-Girl has made me feel kind of special, you know?'

'But you'll always be the Sea-Girl,' Twm reassured me. 'Who knows, there may come a time when you may need to recover the Signs again—and if we return them, we'll know where to find them, won't we? And they'll be safe from the Spoilers. Don't forget, there's still Mrs Gwynne-Davies and Miss Critchett. We've won this time, but—'

I nodded. I guess he was right, but I felt kinda down anyway.

We got in the boat and Twm started the engine. I thought we were headed for the Island, but Twm went out beyond it, towards where the long top arm of Wales stretched out protectively across the curve of the Bay. Once in deep water, we had company. A school of porpoises arched through the water ahead of us, like they were showing us the way, and a dozen or so seals kept pace with the boat, their moist, dark eyes watchful, their whiskers glistening with water.

When Twm stopped the engine, the dolphins came, leaping out of the sea in a burst of rainbow spray, scattering crystal droplets on us, smooth grey-blue bodies flashing skywards and diving down, re-entering the water with barely a splash. We were so far from land I could hardly see the shoreline—but I knew I was safe.

Twm stood up, and stripped off his sweater and shorts. 'Come on,' he said, and I dived over the side, then lifted myself up on the side of the boat to get the rucksack with the Signs, and followed Twm's slim brown shape down into the depths.

Down and down we swam, the water growing colder, although I was not cold, and darker, although I could see as well as I could on land. I breathed easily, knowing I could, and laughed for joy at the lithe bodies of dolphin, seal and porpoise dancing patterns around us. Then, far below, I saw the ghostly top of a tower, glowing pink with phosphorescence, its sides weed encrusted, silvery fish swimming lazily in and out of the tall, arched windows. At the top of the tower a bell swayed gently in the surging water.

Taliesin's tower! I trod water to look at it, remembering

the Legends, imagining the sound that the wind might make blowing in the flute-windows, and hearing in my mind the mellow notes of the great, silvery bell.

Twm beckoned me onward, and at the foot of the tower I met myself.

Well, not exactly myself. It was the girl in the mirror again, her hair darker and longer than mine, her face more pointed.

Her eyes were the strangest, just as I had seen in the mirror glass: large, dark green, with no white surrounding the iris. Maybe living underwater did that, I don't know. Her hair swayed like fine weed in the movement of the tide.

I fumbled with the fastenings of the rucksack—salt water had gotten to the canvas, and they were kind of hard to get undone—but eventually I got inside and took out the Earthstone in its iron box and handed it to the Sea-Girl. She opened the box and removed the flattened, oval stone, the rough, glittering centre catching the faint gleam of underwater light. Next, the Sea-Harp, and lastly the Sky Egg. I gave her the Sky-Egg kind of reluctantly, because I loved it, and it felt like it was mine, you know? But I knew it wasn't, and handed it over. I'd have sighed, but you can't, underwater, without everybody noticing the bubbles, and I didn't want that.

Beckoning us to follow her, the Sea-Girl swam up and up until she reached the top of Taliesin's tower, and we followed her through a weed-hung window. The mosaic floor, although silted slightly with sand, was uncluttered by debris, and the outline of the ornate design was still quite clear. A small harp, intricately carved with flowers and small animals, leaned against the wall, ruined, because the wood had swollen with damp, and weed clung to its strings, but it was still beautiful.

213

The Sea-Girl put the Earthstone beside Taliesin's lost harp, and placed the Sea-Harp beside it, the strings vibrating softly with the movement of the water. I heard the sweet sound echoing in my head. Lastly, she took the Sky-Egg, and went to put it with the other Signs. And then she stopped. She turned round, and handed me the Egg. She did not speak, but I heard her voice, musical as the sea, in my mind.

'Take the Sky-Egg,' she said. 'Keep it safe for me.'

I tried to give it back, shaking my head, but Twm stopped me. 'Take it, Catrin. You are also the Sea-Girl. You should have one of the Signs to keep. It is right. Take it.'

I took it. The Sea-Girl's strange eyes met mine, and we knew each other to be one and the same. And then she was gone, and Twm and I were swimming back up to where the boat, kept in place by the guiding nudges of half a dozen seals, bobbed on the surface waiting for us.

The Sky-Egg was warm between my palms, and its iridescent blue reflected the sparkling, rain-washed sky arching like a blue bowl over my sea.